IN THE
HOUSE
IN THE
DARK
OF THE
WOODS

IN THE
HOUSE
IN THE
DARK
OF THE
WOODS

LAIRD HUNT

Little, Brown and Company
New York Boston London

Little, Brown and Company
Hachette Book Group
1290 Avenue of the Americas, New York, NY 10104
littlebrown.com

First Edition: October 2018

Little, Brown and Company is a division of Hachette Book Group, Inc. The Little, Brown name and logo are trademarks of Hachette Book Group, Inc.

The publisher is not responsible for websites (or their content) that are not owned by the publisher.

The Hachette Speakers Bureau provides a wide range of authors for speaking events. To find out more, go to hachettespeakersbureau.com or call (866) 376-6591.

ISBN 978-0-316-41105-9
LCCN 2018930616

10 9 8 7 6 5 4 3 2 1

LSC-C

Printed in the United States of America

Deep into that darkness peering,
Long I stood there
Wondering, fearing

IN THE
HOUSE
IN THE
DARK
OF THE
WOODS

CHAPTER 1

I TOLD my man I was off to pick berries and that he should watch our son for I would be gone some good while. So away I went with a basket. I walked and picked and ate and took off my shoes. I left them to sit by themselves and tromped my bare feet in the stream. Along I went straight down the watery road, singing and smiling under the sun. The water was fresh and clear and I went farther away from our home than ever I had before. It was nice in the field on the far bank of the stream so I lay down and warmed my wet legs and tried to think of a song as clear and fresh as the water to sing that evening to my son. There would be sweet fish in my song and young frogs and green fronds to wave the good long length of it. Weakness would not be in my song. There would be no harsh word. My man would sit silently and listen.

A noisy band of blackbirds swept over me as I lay there. I leaped up and thought to recross the stream and find my shoes, but the blackbirds had all landed in the trees in the far woods. They were making such a clamor that I thought they were laughing at my bare feet so I ran to them and banged my basket and scattered them away. Into the woods I went, following the birds at first, then finding berries, riper and redder where the sun could catch them at the edges of the glades. Light came spilling down everywhere, and as I stood in one of its bubbling pools I saw at a distance a little girl dressed all in yellow running through the trees. I thought I heard her laugh too but it may just have been one the blackbirds laughing as it flew or a pleasing trick of the wind leaping in and out of my ears.

There in the wood my promise to my man and boy to bring home spring berries to eat with cream from our milking cow came to seem not just a promise I had made but one that I could also keep. This was not a dinner of fat, fresh rabbit for me to ruin. This was not a torn shirt for me to forget to mend. This was not a story whose tail I would take off with my carving knife for having thought of a better one. Fresh spring berries in a bowl. What sweeter end to any story? So I went from glade to glade and bush to bush and plucked and ate and filled my basket. After a time of wandering, I came upon one of the first folk filling a leather sack. When he saw me he dropped all his own treasure and shook his head angrily and pointed back the way I had come. He was small and slight and despite the beetling of his brows had a strange, sweet look about him, so I laughed and walked straight over, lifted his sack, and set it smartly in his hands. I told him that there were berries enough for all who wished to harvest them, and when he set his jaw and shook his head and pointed again, I told him he was just being greedy and that greed was a sin and that if he wasn't careful, God would come to punish him. I trotted away but not toward the stream. It was too early. I did not have enough berries yet.

On I went. A woods can be a miracle of light and shadow. A woods can be a place to dream. Long ago, my father once told me, handsome men and women went to the woods to feast and dance. *I'll feast now and dance later, with my boy and my man, we'll all dance together as I sing my song,* I thought. I popped one fat red berry into my mouth after another. I laughed aloud at the memory of the angry face my fellow gatherer had made at the sight of me.

Presently something pricked my bare foot so I sat to feel at it. Sitting, I realized I was tired. I lay with my feet in the sun and the rest of me in the shade. I pulled my bonnet low. It chafed me so I untied it then I took it off. Two white butterflies flew past. The first of the spring. My man's face then my boy's flashed fast before me. I closed my eyes. I slept.

CHAPTER 2

THE SUN was gone from the glade and gone almost from the world when I woke and took up my basket and went hurrying back the way I had come. I smiled a little but didn't mean it when the oak and ash and box elder began to grow tall around me and my trot turned into a run. There are fears in the airs and on the earth that can call up a fire in your heart whose ash will blacken all hope. This was not such a fear; it was just the little toe or finger of one. I stopped running and wiped my brow and realized I had left my bonnet behind. I shifted my basket from one hand to the other. I stood with my legs planted sturdy and gave a laugh, for I had never liked that bonnet, blue with a frill of tender flowers. A gift from my dead mother.

I took a sniff at the air to see what it would tell me. But the smell was bitter somehow and weak and I could make no meaning of it. There came a crackling as of steps a way off in the dusk light and for a moment I thought it was my fellow berry hunter, but it was not him. It was not my husband and it was not the girl in yellow either. It was no one. I hooked my basket on my arm and thought to say a prayer but found it hard to bow my head and press my hands together, so I set first to walking then running again. When I stopped it was because I had caught a root and had fallen, and as I was rising I remembered I should feel at the trunks of the trees to see where the moss grew best. I felt at one tree and then at another. The moss was scattered thick and cool, and even on the third tree it grew hardiest on one side. But then I couldn't bring to my muddled mind in which direction the moss liked to grow. My man had told me. Had told me in case I was ever in the woods and felt lost. It was a great wide new world we had come to after we had left our troubles behind and he had told me were I ever to wander into its shadows, the moss could help me find my way out again.

Now in its shadows I was. With wet moss tufts at my fingertips. Far from all fair guidance. Alone and now it seemed to me I could hear my son crying through the dark. Weeping for his mother lost. And that I could hear myself, somehow, holding him tight in my arms, crying with him, my cry deeper and longer, almost a howl. Off toward this crying I ran. And realized, when I began to catch speed, that the ground was falling away beneath me and though I liked the feeling of racing downward I stopped because I had not, in coming, climbed any hill. My basket was gone now too. There was little moon and the air seemed made of black butter. Some mist was about. I moved slowly through vines that crept across the course of walnut and hickory. Now and again I stopped, trying to hear what I could hear beyond my breathing. There were bats at work. Bigger things too.

In our new-built barn we had had an owl to visit just the past week and it had chased away the many pigeons that had fouled our sheep and goat stall, fouled our cow stall, fouled the soft dirt over which we came and went each day. The owl had stayed in our rafters long enough to see off the doves and pigeons and then it had left again. My son had found the bones of a rabbit beneath its roost, and my man had hung its skull above the door from a piece of purple thread he took from one of my bobbins and said it would keep the pigeons from coming in again. I laughed at him and earned something sharp when I said I didn't think such work was godly, but so far he was right. Often he was right. No new pigeons had come. Now, here, an owl went its swooping way through the trees and something squealed. My legs were heavy when I heard this squealing, long and loud, so I did not run. I thought I saw eyes off in the darkness, eyes open at the very minute of their own ending, but how could this have been, for there was almost no light in the woods, just the smallest sliver of a moon?

CHAPTER 3

THROUGH THE dark woods I walked, thinking less and less of my son and of my man with his thread and skulls, and of what was godly and what was not, and more and more of my feet, which were bruised and wet with blood. My man, I thought, would have found my shoes and brought them back to the house with him when he started to wonder at my long absence. Or he might have filled them with spring flowers—snowdrops, asters, and sweet daisies—to welcome me back from my walk. Now the flowers would be drooping. Or my shoes themselves would droop, there in a heap with the others, where my man had dropped them by our front door. Dropped them and set the latch so that when I came home I would have to knock. To beg entrance. Thinking of my shoes taken from the stream and lying now in a heap and the door latched against me, I bit my teeth together, breathed hard through my nose, and clenched my fingers into fists. I hit my fists at the sides of my legs. "Don't be weak," I said to myself. I laughed scornfully for having said it aloud. *No need for foolishness so far from home,* I thought. A woman came out of the darkness and touched my arm.

At her touch, all my fine, false courage curdled into a kind of sob and my eyes flared wildly and I have wondered since why I did not leap back when she put her hand on me, leap and run. For here in the flesh was what I had feared most, or thought I had, someone else abroad in the woods with me. Someone with a knife, a cudgel. Someone with nails long and sharp. Still, this woman bore neither of these things, that I could see, and her nails were cut down to the quick. She had a dark string tied around her wrist, a leather pouch slung over one shoulder, and a smaller bag of sailcloth hung from her waist. There was a long, thick scar down the side of her right cheek. Smells foul and fair slipped from her but the first thing that sprang from her mouth was a laugh of her own.

"I am Captain Jane," she said. "And not the ghost you look as though you've seen!"

"What are you the captain of?" I said.

"Of all you see, deary."

"I see only shadows, only you."

She laughed again and said I must come with her, that whether she was truly captain of anything or no, she would pilot me to safe harbor where I could drop my sails, set my anchor, and tend my poor feet.

"Why would you help me?" I asked.

"Are you not lost?" she said.

"As lost as I have ever been in this wood of yours."

"It is not my wood, but I will help you through it just as I have helped so many others."

"Have there been many others?"

Captain Jane touched me again, touched my hand this time. "Come," she said. Her fingers were long and warm, and, though she was not so old, they made me think of my grandmother's, who would sometimes watch me when I was at my littlest, long ago. I had not thought of her in some time and I found some cheer in the memory of her and of her soft, long-fingered hand clamped good and snug over mine as we would walk here or there near the house. I did not much hold my son's hand, which was rough and clammy and touched at things it shouldn't, and I wondered if my man did. Perhaps he did. They walked together well and often enough.

Captain Jane did not hold my hand, of course, but I followed her through the dark woods and when my feet, bruised and torn, began to slow me, she took a root from her small bag and bade me chew it, and before even I had chewed through all its bitterness I felt the pain begin to dull and then fade. My tiredness fell away from me too and whether some stronger trace of the moon had come to trouble at the shadow we swam through or it hadn't, it seemed to me that I could see better and farther, that my eyes, always strong, had become lanterns to pierce the dark. When I told Captain Jane this, she smiled over her shoulder and said it was a powerful root, one plucked from deep soils that had never seen the stars. Roots such as these had been sought after by kings to give to their queens but had only rarely been found. She was making a study of the underparts of the earth, where secrets grew.

"Are you an herbalist, then?" I asked.

"I have walked these woods for a fine many number of years now and made a study of such things even before I arrived," she said.

"You gather at night?"

"Only at night."

"You walk with the ghosts, then."

"But am not one myself!"

"How can I be sure?"

"You can't, but if I were a ghost it's not here I would walk, for I come from far away, from a village in a valley that lies the year round in shade."

"Do ghosts get to choose where they walk?"

"Some do, some don't."

"You are well-schooled in ghosts!"

"I am well-schooled in many things, my dear."

"I know something of ghosts."

"Do you, now?"

"Don't we all?"

She stopped short, gazed long and carefully at me, said, "How do I know you're no ghost yourself? A ghost washed up on the shores of these woods to haunt me?"

Her look was sharp and serious. She took a step back as if to better gaze. I started to say that I wasn't a ghost, that I was flesh and blood and firm in my step, that I was not gray at my eye, nor dead at my pulses, but she snorted merrily and wiped her nose and gave me a playful shove at the shoulder to show that she was taking all we said in stride and fun. The root was in my head and I had forgotten my feet entirely and I smiled at my own confusion and gave her a sturdy shove back. I asked her other questions and she answered them, sometimes by nodding, sometimes by winking, and then there was a silence between us and into this silence a wolf howled.

"It chills the blood," I said.

"As it's meant to," she said.

"My man shot a wolf when we still lived by the sea. Which is where I would walk—by the sea, I mean—if I were truly a ghost and could choose."

"Out over the waters, on top of the waves?"

"And down below, where shells grow slow and sailors sing in their graves."

"There is no sea where I am from."

"Where would that be?"

She pointed off into the dark distance, then let her hand drop. Another wolf howled as her hand touched her thigh.

"Has your man killed other wolves since that first one?" she asked.

I shook my head for I did not know. He was often away from

13

us with his gun. Sometimes he came back with good meat, deer butchered on the trail and carried to us in bloody bags. Recently he had brought a brace of pheasants. He loved best to eat the birds of the forest. He said that after he ate pheasant he could fly in his dreams. He gave the prettiest feathers of the birds he shot or snared to our son, who sometimes made me string them in his hair. I have never liked to eat wild birds. Their meat lies too thinly on the bone. My man rarely spoke of his trips abroad. He rarely spoke anymore at all.

"I have a wolf cloak now to wear when it is cold," said Captain Jane. "There is nothing warmer. I have it fresh from its former owner. She will miss it terribly but it is mine now."

"Did a wolf give you that scar on your face?"

"It was not a wolf."

"We ate the wolf my man killed."

"Did you wear it afterward?"

"My husband traded the pelt."

"A shame."

"The meat was fine and fat. I didn't expect it to be."

"I have eaten wolf too. Of course I have. I have eaten so many things."

"It was a hard winter. Even with the town nearby we were down to boiling bones and boiling them again. I was carrying my son still inside me. My son was born, my mother died, and we left to come to this part of the country soon after."

The wolf howled again and another, nearer by, answered it.

Captain Jane smiled over her shoulder and laughed, and I saw a light through the trees.

"Here we are, deary. Here we are, you poor dear," she said.

I had thought Captain Jane was leading me to her own house and that I would soon see her wolf-skin cloak hanging on its wall, but she turned as I started forward and began to stride back into the trees. I stopped and called after her but this time she did not turn, said only that I would see her again, that Eliza would care for me now if I would only go and step through her door.

"Eliza?" I said.

"It is a common enough name!" The voice that said this came from the house. It was high and handsome. I turned and saw the front door had opened. A woman stood just inside it. She was lit from behind so I saw only an outline of long, buckled hair. I paused and thought of leaving.

"Don't be afraid, Goody," she said.

"But I am afraid," I said.

"Of what?"

"I left to find berries for my man and boy, that's all."

"And what did you find instead?"

I shrugged. I shuddered. The woman beckoned and I went to her. She put a hand on my shoulder and I stepped through her door.

CHAPTER 4

I HAD wandered in the night for such a time that it took my eyes longer than I liked to adjust to the light of this Eliza's fire and candles and lanterns full of oil. It would be dawn soon and she liked to greet light with light, she told me as she bade me sit at a bench by the fire where a small black pot bubbled and steamed. Just as, she said as she ladled water from the pot into a basin and instructed me to place my feet in it, she liked in the evening to greet dark with dark and, fires for heat and cooking excepted, wouldn't suffer any flame to be lit until a day had gone completely to its grave. The water was more hot than warm and my feet were so badly bruised and cut that I cried out when I put them into the basin.

"That's a pretty cry, Goody," said Eliza. "I cry like this." She gave out a sharp sound that made me think first of a fox then of a hawk. Then she put the backs of her hands against the waist of her skirt and said, "No, I think it must be more like this." This time the sound seemed to come from the back of her throat or the root of her tongue, and it was deeper and louder both, like heavy cloth taken in the teeth and torn.

"Make your cry again, Goody," she said.

But I was tired and shook my head, and she said she understood, that it was only a bit of play, for she was in high spirits to have a visitor and had slept well and not walked away the long night without any shoes as I had. She put a woolen throw over my shoulders and said I should rest and she should be quiet and soon the night would slink away to count its accomplishments and day would come.

"It *will* come again," she said.

I started to answer then didn't because I realized I didn't know whether she had meant the day or the night, or in truth what she had meant at all.

While I soaked my feet, Eliza chopped then mashed a smart pile of fragrant herbs she had pulled from pegs on the walls. She did not speak or make strange cries any longer, just sang quietly a little, and, as my eyes had grown accustomed to the light, I was able to look around. The front room of her house was large and neater by far than my own front room with its pile of shoes and my man's gun and the toys he had carved for our son. My man often complained about the state of our front room and about the size of the webs the spiders built in its corners and of the size of the spiders themselves. He had often enough made us both kneel in the dust and beg forgiveness for the sin of my sloth, but there would have been no cause for kneel-

17

ing and begging here. Here everything glistened. Everything gleamed. There were no cracks in the sturdy stone walls, no dust on the well-laid wood-plank floor, no work-worn clothing and soiled rags heaped on the backs of the three chairs. No old food in buckets and bowls. Often I did my cleaning, when I did my cleaning at all, in the night when my man and my boy were asleep and the fire was but a bit of glowing ash and glistening ember. I could work loudly as I liked, for my man's snores filled the house to bursting and there was no one to tell me I had missed a spot and so must beg God's mercy when I hadn't even started sweeping yet. Sometimes I spoke aloud to those snores he made. The answer was always one I liked. "Have you finished with this bit of meat that fell from your beard?" Snore. "Have you brought at last the gold cup and the silver plate you promised I would have when you carried me so far away from my home by the sea?" Snore. More than once I came to stand beside him as he slept and pick crumbs from his beard and stare into his open mouth. He did not like me to do this. He did not like this at all. My son never snored but I stood very close to him in his sleeping sometimes too.

"There!" exclaimed Eliza and I started a little because I had dozed. She was crouched beside me, sprinkling her herbs into the basin with one hand and ladling in fresh hot water with the other. She must have been out in her gardens to work while I dozed, I thought, for there was black at the tips of her fingers and under her nails. I started to tell her that since she kept everything so neat, she could use the water in the basin to wash them, then stopped because I couldn't remember if they had been like that when I arrived.

"Let your sad feet soak a little longer, then I will rub and dress them," she said cheerily. "Perhaps when I do you will cry out again."

CHAPTER 5

WHEN I woke I was no longer in Eliza's big bright room but on a raised pallet in a small room at the back of the house, and I could hear an unhappy pig squealing somewhere beyond its thin walls. I lay still a moment to remember where I was and how I had got there. I made it in my mind as far as Eliza's bench and fireplace but could go no farther. It filled me with wonder to imagine Eliza lifting me up and carrying me into this place. She was slighter by some sure measure than I was. Perhaps I had woken enough to help her guide me here but not enough to remember it. Sometimes my man carried me to our bed, but he was half a giant and despite everything I had always leaped up into his arms. Once at our old home by the sea, to show a cousin that he could, he had carried me in one arm and our son in the other all the way out to the water, where he had dropped us both in. Our son had sunk straight to the bottom. He sat there waving at the emerald weeds with his hands until I plunged down and pulled him up. Not content to let the show stop after the first part of his play, my man made to haul us, wet as we both were, back up under his arms. I said dunking me and drowning our boy was game enough for one day.

"He's not drowned!" said my man, and though I protested, and our boy bit and scratched, my man soon had us back in his clutches.

We all had palms full of sugar when we returned to the house, even our son, though he was very young. Most of his sugar went down his chin and onto his wet shirt, where it glittered. My man's cousin had brought the sugar to us from town. He had brought a pair of chickens in a wooden box and wax for candle-making too. He and my man had fought before the evening's end. They had moved on from sugar to tasting the cider and telling tales with my mother, and the cousin had been whittling the end of his tongue. Ever sharper it grew. My man begged my mother's pardon, then dragged his cousin out the door, said he'd had enough of his gifts and glances in my direction, and threw him off of our property. As I watched, the cousin seemed to go sailing through the air, arms and legs flailing, straight toward me. I saw it clear as that. I started because even when I opened my eyes, I did not think he would stop.

"You have made your cry again, Goody!" said Eliza. She had unlatched my door and come in to stand beside my bed. She was wearing a bright blue dress. There was mud spattered across its hems and there was mud mixed with red under her fingernails and on her wrists.

"Have you been hunting berries?" I asked.

"Berries, dear? Were you traveling in your sleep? Is that what made you cry?"

"I was dreaming of home."

"I dream of home too."

"Is this not your home?"

"Were there mountains in your dream?"

"We lived for a long time by the sea. Often I dream of it."

"In my dreams there are the mountains."

"Tall mountains?"

"Tall enough."

"I heard a pig earlier."

"Yes, I have just killed one."

"But it's not the time for pig killing."

"Is there a time? I wanted to be sure we had fresh meat for a feast. I have leave to kill as many pigs as I want."

She had become ever so slightly vexed or a little worried or both, it seemed to me, as she spoke.

"Leave from whom?"

"You must come and see him."

I sat up at this and stood and, though my feet were bandaged and hurt terribly, hobbled out on her arm. For if there was a host I must thank as well as this hostess, I wanted to do it straightaway. My mother had always taught me to give thanks as nicely as I could, to do it well and quick and to make a curtsy as I spoke. I thought of all the thanks I had given and all the curtsies I had made when I lived still with my mother and even afterward and it irked me—even there on Eliza's arm—some small amount to do so. I had never liked much to bob and smile as my mother had made me do for tinkers, bakers, toothless goodwives, blacksmiths, and even the nameless men who had sometimes helped us with our cows. Still, I put a broad smile on my face as we came around the side of the house and I prepared to dip my head and pull at the side of my skirts. The world has its ways and we do well to abide by them. But there was no host or any sort of a man of the house waiting for me when we got there. It was only a little pig Eliza wanted to show me. Out in the mud of the yard. Still dying of its cuts and not full grown. The knife she had used lay on the dirt beside it. There were half a dozen more pigs of various sizes crowded together in a pen nearby. All of them watched us. I had never seen pigs standing so neatly in a row and barely blinking their eyes. My feet felt like the little pig looked, but I went over to it on my own, took up the knife, and quickly put an end to its loud panting.

CHAPTER 6

ELIZA BUTCHERED better than she killed and so pleased was I to watch her at her work that when she said she would set the offal bucket outside so that she could later rinse it, I stood up quick and took it from her. She laughed kindly as I hobbled off and told me not to hurt myself, but I have ever been sturdy and even with my aching feet I managed. She had told me to set it under a tree in the yard's middle and when I had it there I stood up straight a moment to stretch and knead my back. There was sun and fine thick shadow all around and larks were singing loudly in the trees. What a surprise I had, as my eyes sought to spy one, to find them land instead on my fellow berry hunter, the first-folk man I had seen just after entering the woods. In one of his hands he clutched my basket and in the other my lost bonnet. He held them both up as if he meant for me to have them, then pointed with the blue bonnet into the trees. When I didn't move, he set the bonnet in the basket and gestured with his other hand so that it was clear he meant for me to come.

"Bring them to me, silly, for my feet are sore," I said.

"Bring what?" said Eliza from the doorway of the house behind me. "Tell me and I'll fetch them quick."

I turned toward her when she spoke, then turned back again to the trees and saw that the first-folk man was gone.

"What is it, Goody? What is it you see? You have such a queer look on your pretty face."

I started to speak, but then it seemed so queer indeed to me that he should have been there and then so quickly not that I didn't tell her, said it was nothing, nothing at all.

"It's a funny sort of nothing brings eyebrows fine as yours together so. You would think they were kissing! Come back inside where at least you'll be warm and sitting comfortably if you spy your nothing again."

Eliza cooked even better than she butchered and by the middle of that morning we were eating oatcakes and neat-cut pork steaks rubbed in coarse salt and sage and drenched in honey. I had more appetite than I had realized and whenever she refilled my bowl I ate it down. When I remarked with a kind of laugh on my own gluttony and said my man would have scolded me for such great gobbling, Eliza said it was natural that I should feel so hungry as I had slept straight through the day after I arrived and straight through the night that had followed.

"Put fresh pig in front of someone who hasn't eaten and he will eat until even his teeth grow tired," she said. "I once placed food before a woman who hadn't eaten in a week and she ate at my table until she cried."

I was interested in the woman who hadn't eaten for a week and wondered if it was young pig Eliza had put in front of her too, but this news about my long slumbers made me pause.

"I must go home as soon as we have finished. My man and son will be mad with worry," I said.

"Do they worry about you when you are gone?"

"I have never been gone."

"Never once?"

I shook my head then paused and scratched at my scalp to think if it could be true. It was. My son had woken every morning of his life under our roof to find me near.

"My man travels away from time to time," I said.

"Most men do. Though not mine."

"Why not yours?"

"He likes his land. Its folds and fields suit him. He's like a raindrop that strikes a pond. There, to be sure, but you'll never see it again."

I looked around the room as if her raindrop man might be somewhere sitting quietly. If she saw my gaze and gleaned my meaning she gave no sign. *He's ill abed or off away on some work in the near woods,* I thought.

"My man is happy too. At least sometimes," I said.

"And well he must be, with you for his lovely goody. How old is your son?"

"Six in summer."

"He is young still."

I put another bite in my mouth. Then another. The honey was delicious, heavy gold with marks of comb and only here or there a leg or wing or who knows what else that had been pulled into the trickling swamp. Eliza said she had gathered it from a hemlock hive not far from the house. I knew she must keep a cow somewhere because the feast came with cool, creamy milk. This made me think again of my berries. And of my promise, called out loudly to my man and son as I had left with my basket: "I will soak your mouth in sweetness when I return!"

"You are young yourself," I said.

"Not as young as you, Goody."

"I must go home when we have finished our meal together."

"Straightaway home?"

"I cannot linger."

"It must be very pleasant where you live. You must miss all that you have made there."

"My husband has said that one day we will ring our house with roses and take our drink from golden cups."

"And does he keep his promises, your good man?"

"As much as any other. We both do."

"Then of course you can't linger, Goody," said Eliza. "Of course you can't."

We ate more then, in silence, and after we had finished I sat again on the bench by the cooking fire, which was banked low against the warmth of the afternoon to come, and watched as Eliza packed food for my long walk home. From time to time, I pressed at the floor to see how it felt against my feet but doing so made my eyes water so I stopped. The woods would have softer floors and I could pick my path carefully in the daylight and so the rocks and roots would not hinder me, I thought. I would cross the stream and gather up my shoes, if they had not been gathered, and, latch or no, my man would scold me then smoke his pipe and listen as I told him of my adventures in the woods. My son of course would cry and cry. For fear. For love. For fury. He was not yet traveled far into the journey of words. Indeed, I had never known or heard of a boy to arrive at speech more slowly. Sometimes my man would grab him hard and see if he could shake free any smart-shaped sounds. I was glad enough that this made my small son laugh even though it was perhaps not meant to. Often these shakings ended with both of them fallen on the floor and our small house raw to its roof beams with laughter. I did not join them as they laughed. I sat silent. Still, it did not much matter if my son was quick or dull, as he would work the rest of his days in the stony fields. He would work bent to the plow and walk bent with his weapon for hunting in the woods. He would gather up the ages and plant and reap what he and his father had sown. All the while I would watch. From my chair. From my window. From my garden. Watch until my eyes died at their roots and I fell cold silent in my skirts and could watch no more.

"Here is food for your walk home," said Eliza, handing me over a fat bundle.

"But that is far too much for the journey of a few hours and I have only just feasted at your table," I said.

"Then you can share it with your lovely man and your lovely son when you have joined them."

There were, it seemed to me, a few fine flecks of metal in her voice each time she said the word *lovely,* and I did not like to be rude, so I pulled the bundle in close and nodded and Eliza let the metal flecks fall away and smiled kindly and said, "Now, let's see you out on your way."

"Will you share the start of my walk with me?" I asked as she helped me up and I hobbled to the door.

"Oh, I never leave this house and its fine gardens," she said.

I looked at her because I had been outside and seen no gardens, only yard and pigs.

"You keep your gardens elsewhere?" I said. "And your cow too?"

"They are down the path and near the water, where I'll take the sloppy bucket when you leave. How clever of you to know I have a cow!"

"Perhaps it's tending her each day turns your nails so dark."

She looked at her nails and laughed.

"What sort of water is down your path?"

"Would you like to go there now, Goody? I would be most happy for you to see it."

I hesitated, for I had always loved the water and had missed it since we had come away from the waves and into this land of streams and woods where the first folk kept their kingdom. They came sometimes to our door and gave my man tobacco in exchange for cider. One of them gave my son a doll made of corncobs. My son took the doll and straightaway tore its head off and the first-folk woman who had given it to him beamed so I did not have to punish him as I had thought I must. We had known first folk, of course, by the great waters of the ocean, but they had not been numerous, as our soldiers had chased them and many of them had taken ill in recent years and died. They had not died in any great number here, though. We could often smell the smoke of their fires when we worked the field or gathered wood for our own. Sometimes we heard their cries in the woods, and my man said he found their tracks and traces all about. My man said we smelled their smoky tracks and traces because they wanted us to. It meant, said my man, that we had both the Lord's leave and theirs to live where we did, so close to the great wood. I often liked to think where their tracks might lead, what fine secrets burned at their farthest reaches. I told my man one night when we were all three happily eating a pheasant I had cooked quite well that I would like to follow them and see where they led, and he said firmly that if I did such a thing it would be the end of me and that we should all three pray, and so we did, that such a thing would never come to pass. *Well, wise husband, I have seen one of them at work with berries and had him come again to see and help me, and here I still am,* I thought.

Eliza was clearly not offering me a look at the ocean, even if I imagined for a thrilling moment that she was, but just the sight of a lake, grand and rippling, cool and fresh, would have been welcome. Still, I had been gone from home too long. Perhaps, I told her, someday I could come back to visit her again.

"Then you can see it when you come back. You must come back. You *will* come back. There is so much to see. I can show you my herbs. I have herbs for everything. I have herbs enough in my garden to cure the whole sick world!"

"Is it your herbs that are on my feet?" I asked.

"They feel better, don't they?"

"They do! Thank you. Which way shall I go?"

"I don't know, my darling."

"Then perhaps you can point me to Captain Jane's. She can lead me."

"I've never been there."

"But why not?"

She shrugged. I said I wished I could follow the first-folk man who had come to me that morning with my bonnet and basket, that perhaps he could have helped me find my quick way home.

"A man of the first folk, you say?" said Eliza, her voice darkening.

I nodded.

31

"I wish you had told me."

"Aren't these first-folk woods?"

"Not in many a year."

"But I thought all this country was theirs."

"Not this woods."

"He was hunting berries like I was and only meant to help."

"I'm sure he did. Perhaps you will meet him again as you go. Perhaps he can guide you to your home. Perhaps hope will bring him to you. Hope brings many things." Eliza's voice lightened as she said this, like some dark bird had lit upon it then lifted away again. She smiled more brightly than ever, then leaned over and gave me a kiss. She kissed me on the mouth and made a loud smacking sound as she did so.

CHAPTER 7

I WENT straight off in the direction it seemed to me Captain
Jane and I had come, and although I moved slowly, I was soon
deep among the trees. It was a fine old forest of box elder
and red maple and hornbeam and black birch. For shrubs
there were speckled alder and smooth sumac swaying its sharp,
frondy fingers in the breeze. There were cardinals and jays
aswoop between them to preen and eat at mosquitoes, and
wrens sat calling out early-spring songs in the pepper bush. I
could see from its leavings that a fox had been at work in the
night, and I couldn't take more than a few slow steps before a
black squirrel would poke out at me and scold, which reminded
me of the first-folk man and his insistence. It was nice to be off
and on my way at last with my stomach full and more food at
fingers' reach if ever I felt it wasn't. Only my feet hurt badly
and with every step I took, they groaned. I did not like to look
down at them but I did sometimes. Eliza had wrapped them in
her herbs and rags. Blood was seeping from the deepest cuts. It

looked from the height of my eyes like a rat or weasel had been gnawing at them. My toes peeping out were yellow and blue. I could not believe that a simple walk through the woods without my shoes could have done this. How could it have hurt me so?

I had walked bad-hurt before. Once in my middle girlhood I was kicked in the ankle by a gelding. The blow was halfhearted but it cracked my bone just the same. My father, who was not well that day and could not lift me, had me hold an ash stick and hop and struggle with his help all the five miles home. I had not walked easily for some months after that. Often as I lay resting, my father would come and sit beside me and tell me stories about dancing in the woods or sailing on the sea. He died some years later of a cough that clambered up into his chest. Not so long after, my mother caught her own end. We all go to our ruin. We are all the same in this.

I gave a shiver there among the trees at the thought of my mother lying still at the end of her story. She had been just as big as my man. Just as heavy. Just as strong. Once I had measured the thickness of her arm with a piece of twine. I looped it around the fattest part. By the shoulder, near the socket. I used the same twine to measure my man's arm in the same place after our wedding night when he lay in his snores beside me and it fit just as snug. One day I would measure my son's arm. How thick would it be? Often my man said that when he was my son's age he had been twice as tall. I did not doubt it. I had never tried my father's arm with twine but knew, as with my own scrawny bone sticks, I could have wound it more than twice around.

After what felt like many minutes of walking, I stopped. I thought of calling out to Captain Jane or the first-folk man or anyone at all but could not make my lips move. Instead, I settled myself with my legs crossed beneath a sweet spire and put down my bundle, which had grown warm with all my traveling. I had been taking my course from the sun and its shadows, but the sun had gone to hide behind the clouds. Thinking of my father and my mother, the weak and the mighty, had soured my mood, so I whistled a little and found a tune I liked. I realized it was one of Eliza's, from just after my arrival, when she had stood singing quietly in her front room. It was a tune we all of us with ancestors born far away knew in the world of those days, a simple thing as you would have thought, but its words came to me in a jumble. "As I step forth... A garment fair... A dagger bare... Her golden hair..." As I whistled and tried to call up its words, a cheeky little robin redbreast dropped onto the ground some few feet from me and began to hop and dance and chirp so happily I thought he must be some glamour of the woods. He pleased me so much that I opened up my bundle, thinking to break off a piece of biscuit or some bread. But no matter how far I unwrapped my bundle all I found in it was pig, slices thick and thin. Haunch meat and loin. Trotter and tongue. A kingly gift of meat, but a queer idea for a traveler's lunch.

Still, there was a hungry young bird before me, so I tore off a bit of fried flank and tossed it to him. He pecked it up and chirped for more. That seemed greedy so I called him a greedy guts and told him in jest that if he wanted more, he would have to give me one of his pretty feathers. As quick as you like he pecked hard at his own tail and ripped out one of his feathers with a tug of his neck and dropped it on the ground before me. Amazed, I tore off another piece of meat. Another. The bird ate and ate, then opened his wings and, without any trouble, away he flew. Tearing off the meat had made my mouth water and I put my fingers to my lips and licked at them, but my stomach was still full from my feast with Eliza, so once my fingers were cleaned I closed up my bundle again. The sun was back from its hiding place and I could see my shadow trail. No more whistling. I picked up the robin's feather, which was edged almost to its dark tip with white and flecks of orangey red, and stood and hurried along after it as best I could.

Up through the woods I went and was happy because I could remember my dark descent of two nights before and knew I must be on the right path. "Little robin, little robin," I called cheerily from time to time, but he never came. A crow took his place. It landed on a branch before me, and I thought, in my happy mood, to follow along after it, as I had earlier the great gang of his blackbird cousins, for it seemed willing to lead, but after flying before me from branch to branch, it dropped down quickly from the heights and startled me greatly by flapping and cawing in the sunlit air in front of my face. It might have kept this up or I might have struck it away, only I looked down and saw the pretty little robin's feather peeking out from my pocket and said, "Is this what you want? Is it this that caught your beady eye?" I took out the feather, and indeed the crow flapped its wings once more and landed on a moss-covered rock.

Slowly, carefully, I held out the feather. Sure enough, the crow reached over quickly with its beak and took the feather and when it began flying again from branch to branch, I started following, and I thought that by granting my request as I had granted his, the little robin had not only offered me cheer but given me the gift of good guidance. I thought this happily for some time as I followed the crow but then, of a sudden, the treacherous thing waggled its wings, looked jauntily down at me, and flew off with the robin's feather tucked safe in its beak. Still, it was early, and all I did as I watched it fly away was laugh and then, still laughing, I set off once more. Even when the earth began to drop—and I thought it strange for it to do so because this time too I could not remember having done any climbing—I did not concern myself, because we cannot remember everything. Especially not when we have taken a fright and are running. Have left our home and lost our bonnet and berry basket and are flying barefoot through the starlit woods.

My old grandmother, my father's mother, she of the sweet-fingered grip, had gotten turned around in the mists of age one day and had fallen over and not been able to make her way home. Fit as a sweet-strung fiddle one moment, broken and bow-less the next. Before she fell over, she had often taken me out to dig for clams on the shore. She had laughed and talked and pointed to sails on the horizon. She had asked wouldn't I like to be on one of those boats and a-roving up and down the coast? Wouldn't I like to fly over the waves and be scoured by wet and wind? The songs she sang were about knots and nets in the country of her birth, and many times on the sand, after she had filled her buckets, she would take me by the hands and dance. After she fell and could not rise and something like sea foam spilled from her lips, she had sat for many a month in our house until my mother grew tired of the mumbling and drool-ing and one day, when my father was away, tossed her up over her shoulder and carried her off. I do not know where she took her, nor would either of my parents ever tell me. In the years that followed, it took me sometimes to think I saw her walking ahead of me in the distance, with a bright blue shawl on her shoulders and a long clay pipe in her mouth. She looked—for I saw her striding along with purpose—like she had found her path again and was on her way to the water to dig for clams or board a boat. Because on these occasions I had always seen her in the warm of the afternoon, it came to seem like the right time of day to be walking straight and true.

CHAPTER 8

STILL, IT was in the very brightest portion of the afternoon after leaving Eliza's that I came to a river and felt my hopes sink. For though a stream ran by our house, I had never seen or heard of a river in this country in all the time that my man and son and I had lived there. We did not have many neighbors but there were some and they would come to us or we would go to them so that we could speak to one another of the land and its secrets; of the best season to plant and kill, to sew and breed our stock; of signs in the dirt; and of caves and poison shrubs and ponds and rills and mounds and paths to take and others to beware and the best places to find good honey and where we must never walk alone or unarmed for fear of wolves or bears. No river had ever been mentioned on any of these visits, and yet here, rushing wide and deep, there was one. After a time, though, I thought of the little stream that ran so close to our house, and it seemed plain to me a stream could run into a river and that if I followed the river against its rushing I might yet find my way. That was good thinking, I believed, and my man would be well pleased to hear of it. More than once he had punished me for saying what he thought were stupid or insolent things and more than once he had caught my wrist when I tried to strike him back. My father should many times have struck my mother, if only to pay her in fair kind for all she had dealt him, but I have already told of the size of her arms. When I had come back from our gathering work with my ankle broken by the gelding and no use to the world, my mother had taken the switch to my father for letting me dream of the sea and the wide world beyond it instead of properly minding what I was doing. "She has a right to dream her dreams and fair and many may they be," my father had said just before the air sizzled and the first blow fell. You could see in my mother's furious face that it was as if in contradicting her, he had indeed found the strength to raise up his hand. He was brave for a time that day. Perhaps he was thinking of his mother, my old grandmother, and her fine, fierce ways. It was only after beads of blood began to rise that he ran squealing from the house.

I was standing in the cool of the river's edge thinking so deeply of my mother and her regular use of the switch, which she kept ever near her and which she only ever touched my father with, that I neither saw nor heard the man come running until he was almost upon me. At first he looked so like the father running before the eyes of my mind that as he came crashing through the shallows of the broad river, I thought my reveries had brought him back to me. I was even confused when I did not see my mother on his heels with her switch, striking at him and roaring that I must not dream, that dreams would lead me to my ruin, just as they had almost led her to her own. Even so, that it was not my father became clear enough when the man ran closer and I saw that his eyes, open wide with terror, were as black as my father's had been green. It was the first-folk man, though he held only my bonnet and not my basket now. I took in my breath and opened my jaws to speak but my words stopped short as he went splashing past and, at the sight of me, once again furiously shook his head. He called out something I could not understand then pointed behind him and made it clear that I too should run. I did not run and for a long time after he had gone past I saw nothing, only the rocky shallows of the river beneath the endless trees. In fact, it wasn't until the man had left the river and plunged dripping into the wood and disappeared from sight that I learned what was chasing him.

I heard a low, thick chattering, like thunder chopped thin, and then saw a dark cloud racing over the water. *He has been after honey, pure as Eliza's, and found the hive full of its angry owners*, I thought, stepping quickly back from the water's edge. If this were the contents of a hive, though, then it was the greatest and grandest one ever raised on this globe, for the cloud grew and grew as if to black out all behind it, and the roar even at a distance was so fierce that I dropped flat with my bundle to the ground and covered my ears with the meat of my palms.

41

I thought then to shut my eyes and hope for it to pass me by and leave me to walk along and find my way, but as I gave what I thought would be one last look at the swarm, the sun passed through it and it glittered more brightly and beautifully than anything I had ever seen. It was so beautiful that my eyes refused to blink and were peeled wide when the air went dark as night and the guts of the great swarm came past. While true enough there were bees aplenty among it, there were also great wasps and hornets and fire beetles and moths and flower flies. There were stone flies and mud daubers and dragon-wings and others that I had never seen. The great swarm flew fast along the river then turned hard left after the running man and went cutting with the sound of terrible saws through the trees. I did shut my eyes then, for they had begun to burn. When I opened them at last and uncovered my ears, all was silent. A digger wasp sat on a lump of water-soaked wood by the river a few feet from me. It chewed for a few moments on the wet, dark wood, then twitched its wings and was gone.

CHAPTER 9

ALL THE rest of the afternoon I followed that river until I came to a high cliff and a falls and had to turn away. As the dusk crept over the earth, I chose a stony path and wound my way again into the deeps of the woods. Evening birds flashed across the path. I looked as closely as I could but saw no robins, no crows. So I walked and walked and when the light left, I heard crackling and low voices behind a stand of nearby bushes. I froze and as I did four figures came out. They were dressed in rags. One of them wore on his ankle the remains of a shackle. He walked almost as poorly as I did. The one in front let him hold on to her arm. As I watched, they were joined by a fifth figure. This figure whispered to them and led them forward, and as they hurried off away into the dark all together, I saw that the figure was Captain Jane. Too late I thought to call out to see if I might go with them at least some short way. Instead I stood silent and watched them vanish. As I did, it took my fancy that a sixth figure joined them, dashed at them out of the trees to run in a circle around their group: the little girl dressed all in yellow I had seen when I first stepped into the woods.

Two times since we had moved to this wild country and built a house and a barn and raised up pens and fences, we had had folk on the run at our door. The first time it was a small man with white hair who took the egg and cheese I gave him with a courteous nod, then asked me if I would like to hear a song or a story in fuller thanks. I chose a story, for I have always liked to hear them and think afterward on how they are made, but my choice did not please him and he walked off quickly and would not stop even when I called after him that I had changed my mind and wanted the song. The second time it was three women, each one taller and broader of shoulder than the next, the last one almost as tall as my mother had been, though much finer of figure, and when my man, who was there on that occasion, told them they could not stop at our door, they did not move and they just shook their heads and folded their arms over their chests when he reached for his musket. After a time of us all standing there silently, he gave them water and salt meat and a packet of dried beans to boil just to see them off. Still the three strong women would not leave until my man had not only made them a map to follow north and out of this country but had saddled his horse and led them some miles along their road.

He came home from that ride in a good humor, which could be seen even at a distance and, when he was closer, through his thick beard, and took up our boy and set him on his lap. He said as I put gamed fowl before him that he had been God's soldier that day. When I asked him if it was being God's soldier that had earned him the bracelet of string and seashell he now wore tied around his wrist and that I had last seen decorating the tallest woman's arm, he did not strike me, as he might have, or instruct me to pray for having doubted him, only took the bracelet off his wrist and tied it around our boy's leg and said it had been sent back with him as a gift for our little man. It was a gift earned, he said, for his good service in guiding those three lost souls down the road. Which was surely what, it seemed to me, Captain Jane must be doing with the souls I had seen in her care.

Though Captain Jane, I thought, would have straightaway made sure any people in grave peril had food to eat and roots to chew and a good path to follow as they went along their way and not let them stand there as my man had. Captain Jane would not have tied a favor from one of them onto her wrist after having made them wait so long for her help. No matter how pretty the favor might have been. I felt sure of this.

Later, as I sat with pig meat in my hands, leaning my aching back against a wild plum whose blossoms glowed heavy and white above me, Captain Jane came to me, wearing her magnificent cloak of black wolf skin. At first she seemed a drift of mist and then a double yard of crepe or silk, and both things I readily believed were before me, for every wood after dark bears the blooms of our bright fancies.

"You have gone out walking again, my poor dear," she said.

45

I could see now the string she wore on her wrist was faded red. I reached out my hand weakly, touched at it, and nodded.

"And look at you now."

"Others have been walking and running in the woods this day and night. I'm not the only one."

"I help those I can. Those who stray into the wood and deserve helping."

"Do I deserve helping?"

"Of course you do, poor thing. How could you even ask?"

"It seemed easy to ask."

"You are tired."

"Some I saw this day were not helped."

"Not all deserve it. And need to be shown they don't belong here. That it is no longer their woods. Not anymore."

"I saw the swarm that chased him."

"I love a swarm. Was it grand?"

"It was very large."

"I well expect it was."

Captain Jane pinched the fingers of one hand together and made them fly, buzzing, through the air. The fingers of her other hand soon came to keep them company. She looked at my hands and gestured that they should join her too but I kept them in my lap.

"I have never seen such a thing. I could never have dreamed it," I said.

"Ah, perhaps I'd have seen it too if those poor souls hadn't come along. What was it made of? Wasps? Dragon-wings? Bee-tles? There is nothing in these woods like a swarm."

"There was another could have helped them in your place. A little girl."

"You saw her?"

"I thought I did."

"Did she run this way and that and in circles like a pretty dog?"

"Yes, just like that!"

"I know the one. I know her well. She came to tell me about the swarm. She made me stop and bend down and she said, 'Bzzzzzz!' in my ear."

"Where are they now, the souls you helped?"

"Well on their way."

"I was on my way. I was on my path home." My voice sounded odd, too bright by far. As if another had put it on like a mask to blow a trumpet through my mouth and sound a farce. I felt like my husband had looked when he had come back with the bracelet.

Captain Jane came close and crouched down beside me.

"You will never make it home on those poor feet. I must take you again to Eliza, I fear."

"Couldn't you take me to your house? Just for the night? Just until dawn? Perhaps it is closer?"

"You are already in my house. But not all find it as fit as I do for rest and sleep, play and work."

"This wood is your house?"

"This wood dark and fair."

"Then yes," I said. "Please take me again to Eliza. For fair as it may be, your house scares me." My strange, bright voice cracked as I said this, no doubt because I had gobbled too much meat and was tired and the wolves were howling in the reaches and, though Captain Jane kept her hands at her sides, the swarm in my head was flying around and around.

CHAPTER 10

I WAS several days and several nights in Eliza's small room this time. I had caught a chill in the damps by the river, perhaps as I lay in the mud as the swarm swept by, and my feet had worsened and the invisible swarm of a fever flew in through the cracks in the walls and took me far away. More than once as I drifted above the house in the wood surrounded by mud and pigs, I soared over the surrounding treetops and thought I could spy, far off in the distance, the very furnace at the center of the sun. It was so beautiful, so wondrously clear, that I told Eliza of it when I woke and found her dabbing at my brow with a shadow-cooled rag or working her nimble fingers on my feet.

"Have you flown up and seen the sun of the world, Goody?" she said.

"I have never seen anything of its kind before. It was brighter than a dream of heaven. It was the sun within the sun!"

"That's a gift, that is, to see through shadows."

"Oh, yes, I can see through shadows!"

"And through the night?"

"I can see through the bone to its marrow. I can see through life to its harrow. Once I dreamed my mother was a king and my father a queen and saw straightaway upon my waking I was not wrong. I made them each a crown of daisies but when I told them what my dream had been, only my father would put his on."

"My, my..."

"I must tell Captain Jane! I must tell my man! I must sing it to my boy. Fire, fire, fire, fire!"

"And so you shall, my dear Goody. And so you shall."

My fever broke and I ceased such babbling, but still my head spun and still I lay without moving from my bed. Eliza came many times each day without fail, most often sitting on a small stool, laughing and talking and rubbing my feet like the sister I had never had. We spoke of sisters, for she had had one, and I had wanted one desperately to soothe the long loneliness that had burned across my earlier days and scorched them still. My mother had carried and birthed and lost five children before me and two after, and when I whined to her that I would like a sister, my mother would say that my father was to blame for the barren row I found myself in, and that all I had to do if I was lonely was go to the graveyard and play with the ghosts. I did not like that suggestion and was as unhappy with my mother as one can imagine for making it, I told Eliza, who nodded and said that in her experience, mothers often said cruel things. Eliza's mother, for instance, had once told her after she, Eliza, had made a complaint about the size of her feet that she could quickly solve the trouble of their size by chopping off her toes.

"My mother liked to beat my father," I said. "She once told me that it gave her greater joy to do so than anything else, that it lit the winked-out stars and set the tilted trees aright. Men who beat their women were as common as hard crust on comfort jars, she said, but women who beat their men were as rare as rubies in the wilderness and must be treasured. She said this at table with my father sitting close."

"Was she like you, your mother?"

"We were nothing alike."

"But could she see things clear like you can? Could she see straight through you? See through your hair and skin to your blood and bones? Did she ever give your cheek a lick to see how you tasted and tell what you would become? Did she have a scar on her chest like a door? Did she ever leave you for long periods? Did a squirrel ever come and sit on her shoulder and whisper in her ear?"

"I don't understand."

"And I'm only having fun, dear Goody. My mother never beat my father, nor could she have if she had cared to, at least not in front of me, for he was dead of a quail bone in his breath pipe the week before I was born."

I told Eliza I was sorry she had never known her father for he might have been a good man, like mine had been, even if he was so weak. She said that her own mother had never spoken of her father, beyond occasional mention of his inconvenient dying, and would not answer any question about him put by either herself or her older sister, Glory. Glory had been pleasant enough—though like many sisters she had sometimes held her down and pulled her hair and scratched her and spat upon her face—and they had often played games together. I told Eliza I would like to hear about the games, and Eliza said that we could play. I said I did not yet feel entirely well, but Eliza said there were games that could be played without much thought or moving. When I said I would very much like to try, she clapped her clever hands, then ran off to fetch a mirror.

It was small and round and set in a worn, wooden frame and had a handle carved with leafy growth. I had used a mirror before but not in some great while, for my man could not abide them for the vanity he thought they fueled and had willfully broken the little mirror I had had from my mother who had had it from hers even though he knew it would cost him in fortune and dampen his luck.

"My luck has already been dampened," he said, pointing around us at the wilds we had come to, and of course I could not disagree with him.

The game was called What Do You See? and to play it, Eliza told me, you shut your eyes, took hold of the mirror, then opened them again.

"But if I hold the mirror before my face and open my eyes, I will just see my face and where is the good fun in that?" I said after Eliza had explained it.

"You must not speak for a hundred count after opening your eyes," she said. "After the hundred count is done and if your eyes have stayed on the mirror, you may speak and discover then what it is you have to say."

I repeated my doubts about the fun of this game but sat up in bed, closed my eyes, and accepted the carved handle when Eliza touched my palm with it. I liked its weight and took a moment to run my thumb first along the handle then up in a series of swirls over its smooth back. Then I held it in front of my face, lifted my chin a little, and opened my eyes. I gasped a little at first for I did not look at all the way I remembered myself from staring sometimes into pools or polished stone or dark bowls of still water when my boy and man were away from the house. My face was smaller and neater, for all it looked a little worn, and my nose straighter and my forehead smoother. The hair that fell about my face was long and delicately ringed and pleasantly golden in the room's dim light. *I am handsome!* I thought, but when Eliza noted that the hundred count was done and I might speak, I found myself telling of pigeons and owls and insects and knives and cords for binding and words of fury and the rabbit skull my man had hung at the barn door with my purple thread.

"You see, Goody!" said Eliza and clapped again.

I told her I was astonished for I had meant even until the opening of my lips to speak of my face and how pleased it had made me to look upon it. My fairness as a child had ever worried my mother. If someone remarked upon the sheen of my hair, she cut it off. If someone said my teeth shone lovely, she told me to keep my mouth closed the next time I went abroad or she would reach into the hearth and rub them black. When the dress she had made me came to fit too closely and the eyes around me became too hungry, she tore it off me and made me wear a sack. She had given me the mirror to ensure I stayed plain and said I must never pinch at my cheeks or bite at my lips and I must take in slow breaths whenever my color rose. Once a woman at market in a wide-brimmed black hat to which she had pinned a single deep red rose turned her head to me and told me I was a lovely thing. She held my gaze longer than I could bear and when my cheeks began to burn as red as her rose, I bent my head and thanked our Lord that it was my father and not my mother standing there.

I told Eliza that she should try it, that we should see what she would speak of instead of her own lovely face, but she grew quickly quiet and would only take the mirror from me to set it aside, then she turned the subject to other games she and her sister had played. I begged her to take her turn, but she told me instead of a game called Change About, a game that we could try when next we saw Captain Jane, for it was best played, this game, with as many players as possible.

In Change About, she said, each took a part in a common scene and at a given moment switched. There were different ways to play it. In one, you could switch in only one direction so that once you had had one part, you could never have it again. Hansel could be Gretel and Gretel could become the old lady and the old lady could become her oven and bake all the children of the world but no matter how tasty they were she could never be the old lady again. In the version she and Glory had liked to play, they changed back and forth many times. Their favorite had been the game of the wolf eating the little girl. They had gnawed on each other's ribs and gobbled each other's entrails and torn out each other's hearts. Sometimes their mother had agreed to join in and so the hunter—who got to the girl in time, or perhaps didn't—could be a part of the game. If friends or cousins were available to play, then there could be a grandmother to lie in the bed or rabbits or ravens to look on from the high grass or in the branches of nearby trees and villagers to help the hunter. It was such fun, said Eliza, to be first the little girl getting herself eaten, then the wolf doing the eating, then the hunter the killing, then the rabbit or raven screaming murder, then the villagers going for their torches, and to get to call out "Switch!" when the game was well along. If you grew tired, you left the game and went and sat on the side or the others picked you up and threw you in the bushes or made you climb a tree.

I said it sounded like a grand game and that I would like

to try it when I was feeling stronger. Didn't she wish, in the meantime, though, to take her turn with the mirror? When I mentioned the mirror again she picked it up, touched a little at its back and handle, put it down again beside me, and left the room.

I felt enough myself the next morning to creep out of my closet and into the front room. As soon as she saw me Eliza stopped her work with a scrubbing brush, exclaimed with pleasure, and led me to the bench by the fire. She told me to sit and rest for she could see that while I was better, I was not yet full strong. It was true that my head had already begun to turn and the room with it as I had stood there in greeting and I was glad of the bench and the table behind it to lean against. Eliza asked me if I was hungry and gave me a cup of thin broth before I had answered. I hadn't thought of eating in some long time but sipped a little at the broth while Eliza brought a blanket over to wrap around my shoulders. I was not cold, exactly, there by the fire in her fine front room, but I had been shivering.

"You are so very kind to me," I said.

"Of course I am, silly, for we are friends!"

"I have never had a friend."

"Can that be true?"

"Only animals and dolls and sometimes my small son."

"Well, you have a friend for certain now!"

She went back to her scrubbing as soon as she had me settled and I drank at my broth and looked at the fire, which was small but tight-packed and hardy, like a springtime fire should be. *Sweet fire,* I thought. For I realized fire too had always been my friend. How many times had I spoken to it, murmured to it, told it my secrets? My husband and I had always agreed on the subject of fire. If I asked for a fresh log he always knew what size and shape I had in mind. If he asked for kindling I knew what weight of it to bring and what kind would serve the moment best. There is pleasure real to be had in keeping just the right fire. He and I had frequently spoken of it. Often, when he returned from one of his trips abroad, after we had knelt and prayed together, he would tell me first about the fires he had lit for himself, about how well and long they had performed. Sometimes he stopped at the remains of a first-folk fire and studied them and then told me what fuel they had used and how they had piled it and how brightly it would have burned. It was true that I liked to build the fire in our hearth bigger and brighter than he did, but he never stopped me and sometimes even shared my laugh or smile as I filled our little house with heat. A small fire was just as nice.

As I sat there, I told Eliza about my husband and the matter of fire and of fires, complimenting her as I did so on how she kept her own. I told her that neither I nor my man would have built ours differently. She had chunks of well-cured maple wood and some of oak at the ready should she need them, I noted. She told me that even when I was down with fever I had a falcon's eye for things both near and far. She scrubbed at her floor and at her walls and said that her own husband had been no use at all when it came to fires, that he had always waited for her to light them and when he was alone did as often as not without.

"Is your poor husband dead, dear Eliza?" I said.

"Dead?" she asked. She stopped her scrubbing and sat up to think, it seemed, about what I had said. She leaned forward a little and wrung out her wet towel over a bowl.

"My husband isn't dead. Or at least, not that I know of. Granny Someone says he's not."

"Granny Someone?"

She shrugged and nodded as if this were the name of a friend she might already have mentioned, one that we had discussed and that I should know. "Our home was far from here. As far as your old home by the sea. Didn't I tell you I was from the mountains? In my dreams, at least, my man and my home are there still."

She grew quiet. I had come almost to the bottom of my broth cup when she spoke again. Her words took me by surprise.

"You must see my cellar!"

"Your cellar?"

"You know what that is, don't you, silly?"

Eliza didn't give me time to answer, just took me gently by the wrist and pulled me up from the bench and out the front door and around to the side of the house that looked not onto her pigs but onto what appeared to be a copse-worth of neat-stacked wood. Not just the maple and oak she had in the house but elm and hemlock and half a cord of ash. I wanted to pause a moment to inspect it, to consider the dusky grain, feel the weight and wetness of the fresher logs, judge the older, drier splits for their readiness to burn, but offering me cut wood and its wonders was not Eliza's aim.

"Come now, Goody!" she said and lifted the heavy door of a root cellar that lay beneath the house. She told me to mind my head and be careful on the stone steps for tricky mosses liked them very much. It was true that the mosses were slippery but the steps felt cool on my still-sore feet. The smell of stone and earth and what I thought at first must be rotting leaves that rose around me as I went down behind Eliza made me feel strangely calm. The low roof was hung everywhere with hard, dried meats and strung apples and pears and bunches of sweet marjoram, dill, and sage. There were trays of dried turnips and carrots and casks full of brined squash, beans, and cucumber. There were sweet potatoes, peas, and pumpkin and, on shelves along the far wall, the stripped, stacked bones of chicken, deer, and pig.

"For broth like the one you've just been sipping!" Eliza lit a candle stuck to a barrel of salted eggs and made me sit upon a stool.

"We're just below the fire here," she said as if in answer to a question I had not asked, "so it's warm in winter and cool in summer and it's quiet and the pigs don't call out to me when I'm down here. With my candle lit, I can close the door when it rains and stay snug." Eliza looked at me and I at the room. I thought that emptied of all its great stores, it would seem quite large, larger and finer by good measure than any root cellar I had seen.

"But what do you do in here, Eliza? Why do you come?"

"Ah!" she said. She stood up straight, pressed her thumb and her forefinger together, and began wiggling them through the air. I thought immediately of Captain Jane and of the swarm and looked fearfully into the deeps of the cellar to see if there were hidden hives. I saw a crack in one far corner and worried for a moment that the whole house was a hornet's lair but all was quiet, there were no winged comings or goings, and Eliza made no sound of buzzing as she moved her fingers as Captain Jane had.

"Can you guess, Goody?"

I shook my head.

"Try!"

Her hand moved once more through the air, but she made larger movements this time and then I knew what it was she was doing and caught my breath and thought that if she only moved more slowly, I might follow her lacy loops and lines.

"What am I doing?"

"I dare not say."

"That it's letters I'm shaping in the air and that it's writing I do down here? Of course you can say that."

"In my house, writing is forbidden."

"Reading too?"

"My man sometimes reads to us from the Holy Book."

She gave a laugh, then turned and opened a great chest I had guessed might be full of potatoes but was not. I had never seen anything like this. The chest was brimming with unbound pages.

"But whose writing is on these sheets?"

"Mine!"

"On all of them?"

"No, not all, but why shouldn't it be?"

"There are so many pages here."

"So there are!"

"Writing is for work and God, Eliza."

"Writing is for many things, Goody."

She dug deep in the chest and pulled out pages I saw after a moment were marked differently each from the other and held them up.

"Listen." She read aloud. "'After that, I was not let to eat for a week and then it was only old cabbage leaves.' And here." A whole page of names was written over and over. "'Mercy. Faith. Glory. Welcome. Thomas. Mercy. Faith. Glory. Welcome. Thomas. Mercy. Faith. Glory...' and so on. And this too: 'I love I love I love I love I love I love I love I love I love...' It goes almost all the way down to the end. Then, see, it says, 'I love the world. I do not love the world. I hate the world. I do not hate the world. I do not hate the world. I do not hate the world. I hate the world. I do not love the world.' It's almost like a song. Or a riddle. Though I've never solved it. What do you think it means?"

I shook my head. I had shut my eyes, for when she had started reading I had grown warmer with each word and now felt so warm and strange I feared I might light the walls around us.

"Open your eyes and look, silly. Otherwise these might just be things I am saying."

First one of my eyes crept open and then the other. Eliza was smiling at me.

"Some of these pages are fouled and some are fair. They've been left behind in the box for scrap to scribble on. Or brought after."

"After what?"

"After it all. Some can't stop once they've started and keep up their scribbling for many a year."

"Who brings them to you?"

"Captain Jane. She leaves them at the edge of my clearing. If I catch her at it we have a chat. Sometimes she says she's found them on the forest floor."

"Marked pages just lying on the floor of the woods!"

Eliza nodded. "Other times she says that she's had them from Granny Someone. Who knows where *she* gets them. She might write them herself. Or steal them from others. I've read every word, every page. Can you read?"

I started to nod but then, not sure if I should answer, stopped and pursed my lips. Eliza put her hand on my shoulder and smiled. I took a deep breath.

"Of course I can read," I said.

"There's no shame in knowing how to read, Goody."

"No shame but God's."

"Who told you that?"

I didn't answer. Certainly my husband had. And my mother. And the reverend at the church we had sometimes gone to. But it seemed to me others must have as well. Farmers in their fields. Shopkeepers in town. Merchants and soldiers stepping down off ships. My father had worked at teaching me my letters for a time when I was a girl but when my eyes had begun drifting over signs on stores and peddlers' carts my mother had said next I'd be writing letters to the Devil and put a stop to it.

"Never mind and watch now," Eliza said. She tucked the handful of pages back in the chest and pulled a long small case from atop a pile of popping corn. Inside this case were goose quill and ink and unmarked paper fresh as cream. She took up a sharp little knife that was also in the case and dressed her quill then laid a sheet of the creamy paper on the barrel, where it glowed unaccountably bright. She squeaked open the ink, dipped her quill, and put the quivery thing in my hand. I had never held a quill before. My father had taught me my letters from a book but the only writing I had done was with charred

63

wood and sticks and a fine-tipped brush made of horsehair. When I hesitated she took it back from me, dipped it again, and wrote her name on the paper.

"Now you," she said and gave me back the quill and this time showed me how to hold it. It took me a moment but soon I too had written *Eliza* upon the page.

"I meant for you to write your own name, silly." She took the quill again and dipped it and wrote, *Eliza, Eliza, Eliza's my name!* She must have seen my lips moving and the scrunch of my brow as I read aloud, and slowly, the line of marks she had made.

"I couldn't read well or write any better than you when I first came here," she said.

"I can do both," I said and took the quill back, dipped it in the ink, and would have written my name as neatly as I knew how to make it, but I had dipped too deeply and all that came out onto the page was a great black blotch.

"I can do better," I said.

"It's just that you're tired, my darling Goody. I can see that. We'll come again later and play together at goosey quills. We can tell each other tales with our quills. It's what I do. I write my tale. She's down by the water, the goose who gives these quills. I love the scratch they make. That's the best thing of all. I sit where you are sitting and I make my inky scratch."

"But why write down your tale? Why not just tell it? Tell it over cups of tasty broth? Tell it to yourself? What's wrong with just saying it?"

"Why write it down indeed?" she asked, then took the quill back from me, dipped it, and wrote on the page in big letters beneath my black blotch. It took me some time but I furrowed my brow and moved my lips and when I had worked it out spoke it aloud: "'It's only just for fun.'"

"And fun it is!" she said. She closed her eyes as if thinking of things most sweet and none that were dark and so lovely did she look that I thought it must be so and that what she dipped her quill in and marked her pages with was only ink and not the Devil's blood my mother and then my man had called it. I knew now why her fingernails were always dark. My own were black now too. I shivered and felt my cheeks flush. Eliza opened her eyes and scratched her quill across the page again. This time she was the one who read. "'Once upon a time there was and there wasn't a woman who went to the woods...'

"That's me," she said.

"It's also me."

"Just so. That's the start of the tale. Now, why did she go?"

"Why did she go?"

"Why did she go and what did she do?"

"Went down to the stream and took off her shoe."

"And before that?"

"Set off from her house in a bonnet blue."

"Now, tell me, what did she rue?"
Eliza slapped a fresh sheet of paper on the barrel.
"Is this like the game with the mirror?" I asked her.
She shrugged her shoulders. She handed me the quill.
"What did she rue?"

CHAPTER 11

THAT AFTERNOON, as I sat again by the fire fed by choice hemlock chunks I had selected with pleasure from the great piles, and Eliza went back to work with her brush, I thought about the stool and barrel below us, of how it had seemed snug and exciting both as I had sat there, how though the game was quickly finished, for I was very slow, I too had liked the scratching of the quill, I had liked it very much. Making a song to sing to my boy or ease a long hour was one thing, but this was another. The very sound of scratching as I joined my letters had tugged up pictures and memories like great roots from the garden of my mind. Before we had climbed out of the cellar, Eliza had shown me some of her own neat-marked pages and said that when she was writing them it was like being in the middle of a dream that never stopped, a song that never ended, a painting that was never completed and what could be the harm in that? She said she could tell by my clear letters that I had had some practice despite my fears and the scolding of my husband and I

67

had told her it was true. But a quill on paper was different from a stick on the bottom of a stream or a fingertip on my forearm. Its scratch was like the dry sparking of a flint and a page with fresh marks on it like a blazing porcupine. *A tale written down must be like that,* I thought. It must be like the block of wood of the body sprouting tiny tongues of fire and who knows where the next one will rise and burn.

This picture made me think of a time—soon after I had been kicked and had healed—when I was meant to be working far away with my father and came home to find my mother tearing cloth. She had a chest like the one that held Eliza's pages but hers was filled with wools and silks and linens. She had always called what the chest contained her treasure and she had taken some of it out to show me before, though never to touch, and now she was tearing it apart. There were bits of red and yellow and green and purple and white and black and orange on the floor around her. She had an untorn bolt of dark blue silk draped over her head and wrapped around her legs. Some of the pieces she picked would not tear easily and so she took them in her teeth. They gave a deep, dented sound when they finally tore. It was like a bone under the ax or a stout nail piercing wood. I can hear it now and could hear it then as I sat by Eliza's fire. Our house was always brown or gray, so even with the strange sound of tearing, all this color made me happy. "Mother, you are pretty!" I called out to her from the doorway and then again from the middle of the room but she did not answer, nor even flick her eyes at me, and after a time of watching I took up what I had come to fetch and went back to my work.

That evening when my father and I returned, the cloth was again in its chest. I made to run to it, for I had thought of nothing but color and tearing all day, but my mother caught me up and set me on my chair so hard it cracked a leg. Then she scolded me long and loud. "That's my chest and in it is my treasure and you have broken your chair!" she cried. She shook as she spoke. She slapped away my father when he tried to hush and soothe. Only prayer on the hard floor could calm her. As we knelt with hands raised in special supplication and heads bent so that our chins pressed against our chests, I saw my mother had missed a bit of green cloth beneath the table. I took it up and made to show her but my father's hand closed quickly over mine. He tucked the cloth in his pocket. He shook his head. My mother put a lock on her treasure and my father said we must never ask her to open it, that it was all she had left of the family she would never speak of.

I wonder what she would have said if she had visited Eliza's cellar or one like it, I thought. Then I thought, *A tale is a funny thing, and even when it's your own and you have a quill in your hand you must be careful where you touch it.* Then I stopped thinking because Eliza looked up from her work and surprised me once again.

"A bath's what you need!" she said. "Our talk earlier about my fool husband and my long life here and songs and play in the cellar and this scrubbing brush in my hand has made me think of it. For all his faults he would always give me a bath when I wasn't well. A bath is a wonderful thing. Does your husband give you baths?"

"Never!" I said and almost laughed aloud at the thought of that great brute giving me anything but a scolding or a kiss I hadn't asked for.

"Such a shame . . . it is marvelous to hold your knees in your arms and have your back smartly scrubbed and a song sung sweetly into your ear."

I said that I was satisfied after our time in the cellar just to sit there by the fire and that soon I would need to return to my pallet and sleep, but Eliza said a bath before sleep would make my dreams all the sweeter and that now the idea had come to her she wouldn't hear any argument. She busied herself then for the next long hour in dragging in a great tub—much bigger than the one she had soaked my feet in—and bringing water and building up the fire with more fresh wood and boiling kettles full. When all was ready she had me step out of my dress.

"No wonder you shiver so, Goody!" she said. "We'll have to fatten you up! You're all skin and bones! Look at you!"

I blushed under her gaze as brightly as I had in the cellar and stepped quickly into the tub. I gave out my gasping cry again as I crouched because the water felt so sharp on my aching legs and stomach and hips. Before I knew it, Eliza was pouring water cold and hot onto my back and over my head and down my arms. She scrubbed me then as I had never been scrubbed in my life. She scrubbed me like I was the floor or the walls. Like I was a spoon or a pot. I cried and moaned and gasped as she scrubbed. I protested when she took the brush to my nails, for I liked to see them black, but she said I'd soon have them dark again and for now they must be as clean as the rest of me. She sang some of the time she worked on me. She said her husband had had a fair singing voice, that it was the best thing about him, especially when she was in a tub and wet. He had used it often enough to soothe their children, and it had worked on them like a spell or a glamour or a charm.

"You had children too!"

"Girls. Baby things. They'll have grown now."

"Did they leave you? Your man and your children? Or you them?"

Eliza, behind me with her brush, did a funny thing instead of answering.

"What are you doing?" I asked.

"There is a fine red heart in there and yes, there is," she said. I could feel her ear and cheek against my back. She pressed harder. "It pounds and thumps and wallops and groans."

I leaned forward away from her though there was little room, but her head came straight along with me.

"Oh, it's a merry thing, this heart of yours," she said. "It's like a drink in a small glass on the deck of a storm-tossed ship or a shout in a fiery room."

"Have you heard many hearts?" I said, for with her ear still pressed against my back, my tongue felt heavy and I did not know what other remark would serve.

"Not many."

"Did you hear your husband's?"

"Not his."

"Your babies'?"

"I don't remember."

"Your sister's?"

"Not hers."

"Then whose?"

"It is a great heart, the one I've heard, Goody. It wants the whole world and will have it! It is grand as a castle built with a thousand rooms."

She said this, then pulled her ear away from my back and fell once more in earnest to her task. I asked her whose heart had a thousand rooms, what heart of this earth could be so grand, but she would not answer this nor any more of the questions I asked her, and ask I did, for I felt there lurking some story of lost and broken love that had brought her to these woods, hope gained and hope abandoned, some tale worth the teasing out—perhaps the one she did her goosey scratching on—and thought she might still tell me. But she only scrubbed without answering and sang about moonlight and after a time told me to stand and step out so she could rub my hair and dry my back and get me to my bed.

CHAPTER 12

AFTER MY scrubbing, I slept deeply the rest of the evening and when I woke in the night I thought first not of Eliza and her family and my own, who seemed far away, nor of lovers with hearts like bloody palaces, nor of creamy paper and scratching quills, but of the mirror and what I had said after I looked into it. Soon enough these things—hearts and paper and lost families and the carved mirror—came to seem one in my mind, and presently I lit the candle Eliza had left by my bed, shut my eyes, took up the mirror, opened my eyes, and looked into it. I waited for a hundred count then spoke, but this time I said only what my eyes confirmed was there before me, a face, handsome for all that: a pair of eyes set good and deep in their sockets, a nose that hadn't yet been broken, still-fair teeth, and an unbruised mouth.

Now, my room was connected by a short stretch of hallway to Eliza's, and after I had unsuccessfully played the game without her once more, it took my fancy to surprise her as she slept and ask her again to play or, if still she wouldn't, at least to explain why the game did not work when I was alone. So up I stood, leaving my candle behind, and stepped out into the hallway. My feet called up a lively creaking from the floor, and I thought sure my surprise would be spoiled and half turned to go back to my bed. As I did, though, I heard a moan, just a slip of a sound from the front room, and thought Eliza must be there. I was about to step down the hallway and toward it when, coming from the direction of Eliza's room, I heard the self-same moan. Far from pretty did it sound to my ears that second time.

I am dreaming, I thought, *and should go straight to my bed and hide under its pillow, for, like quills, dreams can mark you, dreams can stripe your back.* Still, I have never been strong at heeding counsel, especially not from myself. My heart beat hard as I went down the hallway and peeped around the corner. There I saw Eliza, sweet Eliza, crouched naked with her back to me in the bathing tub. The room was dim and cold, although the embers of the fire beside her were glowing still, and even a damp log would have brought it speedily back to full brightness. I wondered if the door to the great dark world was open but my eyes could not see far enough through the gloom to tell. I was about to speak, to ask her why it was so cold, to offer to reawaken the fire, when the fancy took me to place my ear on Eliza's back. I would listen to her heart, as she had to mine; I would feel its warmth and count its rooms. So I crept forward, cleared away my hair, and put my ear to her back.

What did I hear? Very little. A faint pulsing, a fly's tongue, a frog's breath. It was like an empty cupboard, a larder bare. Eliza didn't move when I touched her. She was warm and her skin before my open eyes curved in a blur and glistened like the bowl of a spoon in the ember light. I decided that to hear so little I must have wrongly placed my ear—that somehow I was listening not to her heart but to the small bones of her back— and thought to move it when I heard again the little moan from behind Eliza's door. "What could that be? Do you hear it too, Eliza?" I said to my friend's fine back and to her neck and to her damp locks, but she did not answer, did not move her head or lift her arm. So after a time I turned away from her and left the front room and walked down the hallway, which seemed now twice as long.

The door to Eliza's room was not latched and I pushed it open easily. Fearing what I might find, for how could I not, I tightened my jaw and slowly, slowly peered in. At first I could not credit what I saw. There on her back lay Eliza, eyes closed, face turned toward me, lit by a candle like the one I had in my own little room. She wore a gown of simple cloth, open at the neck, and her chest rose and fell, fell and rose. *I am dreaming sure,* I thought. *So what can it matter? It will mark me as it likes, this dream, whether I wish it to or not.* I went forward slowly and stood at Eliza's side and peered at her face and, by and by, let my ear, still damp from the first Eliza, sink slowly to this one's chest. *Here I am closer to the heart,* I thought as I listened, but once again I heard nothing. Or nothing's dearest friend. Perhaps the sound an owl makes as it lifts from a branch or the faint scrape a finger draws when it's pulled across a palm. I moved away and the silence deepened into all its small sounds. The rising and falling of Eliza's gentle breathing. The creaking of the house, the crackling and curling of the night. Presently, I heard the moan again and then another sound. I thought it must be some branch brushing its leafy tips against the side of the house, but then I realized it was weeping. I stood and went to the little window of Eliza's room and looked outside and saw her sitting on a stool. She was hunched over with her face in her hands. Beyond her I could see the pigs in their pen, lined up together as before, each lifting one foot and then the other, as if there were music or the mud beneath them were a drum. I tapped at the window to see if Eliza would turn but neither she nor the pigs seemed to hear me. "Why is she crying? Why are you crying?" I asked the Eliza lying on the bed.

I suppose I would have stayed and tried to put more questions to this Eliza as I had tried to put questions to the other, or pried open the window and called outside, or stepped quietly away and crept back to my room, but then like a bell struck soft but true came the moan again. It came in a chorus this time, from the front room and outside the window, yes, but now also from other places: from down in the root cellar under the wood plank of the floor where Eliza did her scratching, from the ceiling boards, from the chimney shaft, from the walls, even from my own room. *Who is moaning in my room?* I thought. *Is it me or is it Eliza?* Only here I was and here was she. The moaning stopped. "Eliza," I said. But she did not move at the sound of my voice any more than the Eliza in the front room had. "Eliza," I said again, more loudly, and though the shape in the bed before me stayed silent, the moan sounded alone once more.

It came from farther down the hall, from a room I had not yet entered. I took Eliza's candle with me for there was no light or very little by this door. I stood before it for what felt like a long time. At last I pulled at the latch and held up the candle and there lay Eliza curled on the floor. A smell of wet and burning both came toward me. Her eyes were open. She was looking at me.

"You should go and rest now, Goody," she said.

I did not move. "Where are you?" I asked.

"In the house in the dark of the woods."

"Then I've found you."

"Yes."

"I've seen three of you this night and heard a dozen more."

"Only a dozen?"

"There may have been others."

"You can see me, you can hear me, you could reach out your hand and touch me if you cared to. I am where you are, Goody."

"I have heard your heart," I said.

"Was it loud or soft?"

"Soft."

"Ah."

For a moment, her gaze left mine. The room was deeper than I had realized and to see what she saw at that moment I would have had to turn eyes and head and body all.

"You should go now, Goody. Go and sleep. It's so late," she said.

"Let me help you."

"You would help me?"

"It's I who'll carry you this time," I said. "We'll heat fresh water. The tub is there. We'll take you away from here and put you in a fine warm bath." I shivered even before I had finished saying this for I had forgotten that she was already there, already in the front room, already in her bed, already under the floorboards and writing on her barrel and in the chimney and in the rafters and sitting on her stool in the yard, and in the ash of the fireplace long since dead. Sometimes at home, when it was fearsome cold and even a strong fire could not help us, my husband would say a prayer and curl himself around me and I would say a prayer and curl myself around our boy and he would say nothing and by and by we would become almost warm.

"I would try and hear your heart one more time," I said.

"Then come and lie beside me, Goody."

I stepped into the room and gave a gasp for the floor was icy cold. Again the chorus of moans sounded. But much louder.

They hurt my ears. Eliza was gazing into the farthest reaches of the little room. I looked and could see a misting in the air and a slight buckling of the floor. "What is it, Eliza?" I whispered as I lay down beside her. "Quiet now," she said. The moans were all around.

CHAPTER 13

ONCE, WHEN my mother was away from the house, a traveling troupe came to our door and blew on a horn and beat a drum and asked if we would like a play. My father gave them a coin to make one for us. The troupe's leader, a juggler, said for the size of the coin my father had given there could be no play, only a trick or two to tease a smile. I remember a woman who swallowed a sword and another who stood on one hand as her bright dresses fell down upon her face. It was the final trick, though—for the making of which the juggler turned our empty rain barrel on its side and leaped upon it—that returned to me as I lay half wrapped in chilly sleep in my closet the morning after my deep-night journeys around the house. For some moments after he had first found his balance, the juggler rolled the barrel forward, saying he was an angel, and rolled it back, saying he was a devil, and because he stood tall and calm as a statue when he was an angel, and crouched and pulled faces when he was a devil, and seemed always on the point of falling to his doom but never quite did, we began to laugh. "Angel, an-gel, angel, angel," the juggler said, standing tall. "Devil, devil, devil," he growled as he crouched and grinned and winked. At some point he began to say, "Devil, devil, devil," when he was stand-ing up and rolling forward and "Angel, angel, angel," when he was crouched and rolling backward. From then on he changed it back and forth until we were all a-jumble with devils and an-gels, and my father and I were laughing so hard we had to lie down on the ground. Lying there in my room, caught between the dark of sleep and the light of wake and thinking of that juggler on our rain barrel all those years before, I wasn't sure which way I should turn and what I would be and find when I got there. So when Eliza came sweeping in and said cheerfully that I must rise and go out into the world of birds and breezes again, I was slow to respond. "How could I live yet lie abed so long?" Eliza asked me as she inspected my feet. I was clean now and my feet much healed and the place where we could play more games and live like sisters was just outside her door. She spoke then of her gardens and the great water that lay be-yond them, and it was this that woke me, that pushed the night aside and made me think to move. There is a magic in want-ing to see a thing that has been marvelously described and it seemed to me I could see those gardens and that water that Eliza spoke of like they were floating by the bed. There was the cow and there was its clean stall and there were the sheep and goats she said she kept beside it in separate pens. There was the goose she plucked her quills from and rows of new plants and powerful, fragrant herbs peeking up out of the fresh-turned earth. More than once as Eliza spoke ever more excitedly, I rubbed idly at my linens and thought to touch good dirt with my fingertips or cup clear water with my palms.

"You won't need your lost shoes to walk on that soft earth, my darling," she said, and as she said it the blanket of my strange dreams fell full away from me and I could feel the clumps and grains of that softness clearly, for I had always loved to worry sun-warmed soil with my toes.

Later that morning, then, with Eliza's gardens and great water before me and the long, dark dreams behind, I balanced on the barrel of my full waking and went into the front room, where I ate all that I saw of cheese and dried apple and sausage. I ate and ate until I laughed aloud at my own ravening and at my own strange fancies of tubs and silent hearts and cold, hard floors. There was a story to write *and* tell. A woman went walking in the woods and took a bath! I was laughing as loud as Captain Jane when I heard a knock on the front door and laughing when I answered. There before me stood a little girl dressed all in marigold yellow. Her hair was long and dark and she held a pretty, curving piece of jet-black bark in her hands.

"Eliza is not here this moment, young one, though she can't be far. Shall I call her?" I said.

The little girl peered up at me, then smiled shyly and shook her head. I saw when she did this that she had somehow caught a bright-blue beetle in her hair. It was hanging by her ear like a long-armed monkey I once saw come off one of the ships of my youth. I started to lift my hand to brush it away for her but the little blue thing dropped of its own accord, landing first on the girl's foot then crawling off across the yard.

"Where have you come from, young one?" I said. "Do you live in the forest? Haven't I seen you playing in the woods before? Didn't I see you bobbling about Captain Jane just the other evening in the dark?"

The little girl smiled and shrugged. As she did, the robin I had met in the woods before flew out of the trees and landed on the ground beside us and snatched up the blue beetle and swallowed it. Then he began to peck at some pieces of spilled corn.

"I know this little robin!" I said. "We met in the woods. Do you know this cheeky bird?"

The little girl smiled the prettiest smile in answer while the robin gave out a happy chirp, for he had found a fat worm. We watched and the robin set to tugging the worm he had found thick and glistening from the ground. When he had it up and into his beak, the little girl turned back to me and held out the piece of bark.

"Is this for Eliza? Did you find it in the forest? Shall I give it to her?"

The little girl just smiled. Such small white teeth. Such pretty lips. Fine for smiling and frowning both. For whispering what she liked. For eating what she would. I took the bark, held it up to the light. It glittered and glistened. Was smooth on its inside and rough on its out. I brought it to my nose for a sniff, found there an aroma of cinnamon or some other fair spice grown up out of the earth and gathered and sold to tease the noses of us born half the world away. It had a rounded crack large enough to see through at its middle. I put my eye to it and looked down at the little girl and grinned. She grinned back. Through the black bark she seemed to have grown smaller and paler, as if she were made of moon and fed on night and were set to fly away, and the little robin on the ground next to her grew larger and not so pretty and looked at me with a strange and hungry gaze.

"What tree do you think this comes from, child?" I asked as I pulled the bark quickly from my eye, for I did not recognize it, though I knew many trees.

I was not surprised of course when she didn't answer, only gave a curtsy, neat as you like, her grin gone, and peered up at me, her own sweet size again, just her shy smile and the little robin gaming to find more worms in the ground beside her. After she had looked quietly and sweetly at me, she turned and, with the robin following close behind, ran off into the trees.

I watched her run, then stepped full outside, breathed in the fresh air, cast my way about for a moment, then found Eliza behind the house with the pigs. I opened my mouth to greet her then stopped when I saw that she was talking to them.

She spoke for a time then paused and cocked her ear as if she were taking a turn at listening, listening with great interest to the grunts and squeals they made. I stood at the edge of the house with my hand shading my eyes against a red glare coming through the trees and thought it must be a thing most curious to live alone in a wood and that I might come to hold like concourse with my animals if ever I did. I moved my hand to brush away a fly or scratch my nose, I can't remember which, and one of the pigs looked over, then back at Eliza, and gave a grunt.

"Here you are, up and out walking in the daylight on your own!" said Eliza. She stood up from her squat and came striding so quickly that I flinched a little, fearing, of all things, though just for a moment, that she meant to strike me. All she did, though, was lay a pretty hand on each of my shoulders and look me over and tell me my color was much better, that soon I would be shiny as an autumn apple and twice as firm. After she said this she gave me another kiss. Straight again on the mouth. Then told me I shouldn't think anything of a kiss like that, that a kiss like that was the custom for all in her country off away in the mountains. I told her I wasn't troubled, though I suppose I was. Such kisses had certainly not been the custom where I had done my growing by the sea. The pigs behind her squealed at something, and we both turned to look, and I told her I hoped she wasn't thinking of killing another one of them on my behalf.

"Oh, we have meat enough for now. If we grow hungry for fresh cuts, we can kill a sheep or a goat or beg a brace of quails from Captain Jane or Granny Someone," she said.

"Or we could get them ourselves," I said.

She didn't answer this, just turned away from the pigs and looked at me.

"Now, what is that you are holding?" she asked.

"You've had a visitor," I answered.

"Have I?"

"The handsomest little girl. She left this for you."

I held out the bark. Eliza wouldn't take it.

"You can look through it," I said. "It smells clean and fresh and grown far off."

"I know all about that child. Lately her visits have become rare."

"Won't you take it?"

"You keep it."

I shrugged and tucked it away, for Eliza seemed vexed by the very sight of it. Her face had gone red and her breathing had changed. Her eyes had gone smaller and her lips had pursed. She gave out a sigh that sounded as if it had traveled from the very bottom of the cave of her lungs after I had tucked the little thing away into one of my pockets. Eliza's hands went up to my shoulders and she squeezed them.

"Anyway, we'll leave these pigs to grow and fatten properly," she said. "I've just been telling them that. That they must grow fat for us. There is nothing quite so cheery in this world as a great fat pig!"

She hugged me then. Pressed me hard in her arms. I could feel the black bark against my leg as she did. I worried that it might break and shifted so it would bear less of her weight. As we stood there, heart pressing heart, the past night returned to me, but out in the sunshine in Eliza's welcoming arms it soon felt far indeed away. When Eliza had finished with her hugging she stepped back, adjusted her hair, and beamed.

"And also of course I have told them our good news. It made them so happy! Can't you see how excited they are?"

I looked over her shoulder at the pigs but could not see their excitement. They stood close to one another, rubbing flank and shoulder. One of them gave a soft grunt.

"What is our good news, Eliza?" I said.

She looked at me as if she were astonished. She said, "Why, it is the best news in the world!"

"What is?" I said. I laughed a little, though it was no true laugh, for she was looking at me so queerly.

"We spoke all last night about it, Goody. Don't you remember? Has a return of the fever robbed it away?"

"I remember nothing of any talk," I said. "We had no talk. I remember our game with the mirror, then my bath, and afterward my strange dreams."

"What strange dreams, Goody?"

"Now it is your turn not to remember."

"How could I remember your dreams?"

Eliza took a step away from me, straightened her skirts, let some of the curve of her smile fall away from her lips. "What did you dream, Goody?"

I started to speak but found I could not tell her. Eliza felt at my forehead and touched at my pulse. She looked me up and down and, though she seemed satisfied, sighed again. There was something in this sigh and in her strange words about news that made me angry.

"Don't call me Goody," I said sharply.

"But why?"

"Because it's not my name."

"Of course it's not. What should I call you? I'll call you whatever you like."

"You know my name. I wrote it down."

Eliza's smile did not waver when I said this but I saw her eyes flick up and down the length of me and I realized I had clenched my fists. I could feel a pounding pulse in my neck, and my legs were shaking. I brought in a breath but it would not take. I took another and held it, then let it go with a gasp.

"It doesn't matter," I said.

"But it does!"

"Never mind what I wrote. Call me Goody. It's what the world calls me. For I am a wife."

"But I am not the world…"

"Call me Goody. I don't mind when *you* call me that."

"Because we're friends, Goody?"

I nodded. One of the great pigs grunted. I looked over Eliza's shoulder. It grunted again. "Were you called Goody? Before you came to live here in the woods?" I asked.

"I think so. Yes. I must have been."

"And did you like it?"

"I don't remember."

I nodded. For it suddenly seemed such a silly thing to be wasting words or anything else on. The silliest thing in the world.

"Forgive me," I said. "I have an anger that runs away with me."

"Like a volcano."

"Or a crashing wave."

"Or an avalanche of earth and rock."

"It always passes."

"But comes back."

"You understand everything."

"Of course I do."

"Say you forgive me."

"I forgive you."

"What is this news you spoke of and that I can't remember?"

Eliza smiled, dipped her chin, took my hands in hers, and lifted her shoulders. "Our news," she said, "is that you have decided to stay here. With me," she added. "With us," she said, pointing back at the pigs.

"I have what?"

"You have decided to stay."

"I said I would like to play at Change About with you and with Captain Jane. And this morning that I would like to see your lovely garden and the water you spoke of. You are my friend and I have not had another in many a year. But I never said I wanted to stay, Eliza. I cannot stay. I must keep my promise. I must go home."

"But it was decided!" she said.

"It was not!" I said.

The anger I thought had left me had only been resting a moment. I dropped to my knees and, dragging my nails and knuckles, made the word *no* in the yard's packed dirt.

"Can *you* read, Eliza?" I asked. The venom of my words carried clearly across the yard. For when they heard them, the pigs shrieked and began to turn circles and bite wildly at each other and run at the sides of their pen.

CHAPTER 14

ELIZA MADE no shriek of her own but would not speak to me for all of the next few hours, and when finally she came to me where I had gone to sit and drowse beneath a sugar maple on a bed of breeze-worn mosses, it was to hand me a cup of the healing tea she had kept me filled with all the days and nights I had spent with her, even when I had not been able to lift my head alone to drink it. Once the cup was in my hand she walked quickly away.

"I will need shoes this time if I am to make it safe to my man and son," I called after her.

"I have no shoes but the ones for my own feet and may soon need them myself," she called back.

I swallowed the tea in a single gulp, stood, and brushed off the bits of fluff and grass that had settled lightly upon me as I sat. It is one of the oddest things about the world, that it wants constantly to drop something onto you, some small reminder of itself, branch or stone or seed or dust. You might think we were born to become midden heaps and not engines for hosannas and hard work. I followed Eliza with the idea of pursuing the matter of shoes and leaving. She walked faster than I could manage, slow as still I was, but once she had passed the pigpen, whose residents stood in their straight row again but this time only glowered at me, I could see that she was heading in the direction of the gardens she had so lovingly described. So I slowed my step and then, feeling well foolish after my rest for having done it, stopped a moment to kick away the *no* I had written on the dirt. "I never told her I would stay," I felt compelled to say to the pigs as I did this, but they had become interested in some slop in the corner of their pen and ignored me. Leaving them behind, I listened to see if the sound of other, finer animals or the lapping of water would lead me. Animals I could hear, but they were animals of the air and trees. Wrens and cardinals and large red squirrels who clicked and scolded. Still, my man had always told me to walk through the woods with the deep part of my eyes and not the shallow, and by and by I felt I could see before me a path. It ran on through a stand of old spruce whose drooping arms seemed to touch hungrily at me as I passed.

The way turned sharply when I had moved beyond them and as I stepped around a great rock covered in brown moss and orange lichens, I came upon Eliza. She stood, with some light breeze lifting her hair, facing away from me on the grassy banks of a great and lovely lake. There was many a handsome reed around her and red-eyed ducks afloat, and the sight of the clear water, rippled and deep, made me forget for a moment to breathe. In the foreground, paddling back and forth before her, was the goose from which she plucked her quills. It was a great heavy thing and gave a happy honk as it paddled, as if it were glad to see her. Farther off along the banks in one direction were the pleasant pens and peeping heads of all the animals she had described, and the most enchanting beds of early herbs and plants stretched out as far as I could see in the other. I didn't know which way I wished first to turn and so thought I should run to Eliza and take her hand and see where she would lead me. It was all a marvel and I wanted more than anything I could remember to forget our silly quarrel and visit this place with her. And visit it I might have and even stayed for a swim in its fragrant waters only the wind changed or I shifted and felt the press of the child's bark in my pocket. Before I had even a moment to think, I had brought it back out into the air and had lifted it to my eye.

Gone immediately were the gardens, gone the lake, gone the handsome pens. A crow much like the one I'd met in the woods but with half its old, foul feathers plucked was pecking at its own feet, and Eliza was standing, arms outstretched as if in greeting, up to her ankles in a swamp. She still faced away from me, and her hair, which only those minutes before had seemed shiny and sun-filled, now hung dark and damp, and the part of the teeth I could see her give welcome with were a blighted

93

brown. There was a nasty bruise on her cheek. Her nose looked swollen, as if it had been struck, and her clothes were filth-covered and torn almost to rags.

"Come now, even if you are grown weary of me, come to me one last time, for I need to feel the warmth of you for courage," she said, opening her arms even wider, and when her arms moved, it seemed to me, as I peered through the black bark, that there was someone or something just beyond her that her rags and frail body blocked from my view. Worse was the feeling that came over me that whatever thing it was, it was not looking at Eliza; whatever it was, it was looking straight through her at me. I pulled myself back behind the boulder, took two quick steps, stumbled, and came down hard to the ground. As I fell, I flung my arms forward, and far away from me toward the heavy trees flew the little bit of bark. I gave a cry when it did but heard footfalls behind me and dug my fingers into the dirt and stood and half slipped again and staggered sideways and hit hard against the orange rock.

"You will hurt yourself galloping around like that, Goody," came a cheerful voice. It took me a moment to understand that it was Eliza's. A moment longer to dare to look up and see her standing before me, as I knew her, in her smart dress, with her bright, fresh smile, unbruised face, and beautiful hair. Behind her was the grand lake of lapping water and next to the lake were the gardens and beyond the gardens a cow chewing its cud next to other animals housed in sturdy sheds.

"I didn't know you had followed me, silly thing! Come and take my hand and let me show you all that's here," said Eliza.

I didn't move. My wrist hurt. I held it hard against my side.

"Why, look at you!" said Eliza. "You look as if you've had a fright."

"I have had a fright."

"What sort of a fright?"

"I have *seen*."

"Seen what?"

"Last night through the lens of sleep and shadow and through the bark just now."

"What have you seen?"

"I don't know. You won't tell me what this is. You speak of hearts and of him. You should weep for the lie of this place."

Eliza frowned.

"I haven't wept in years. There are no tears left in my head."

"What were you looking at when you lay upon the floor last night? What was there with you? What was at the back of that room?"

"Are you well, Goody?"

"When you lay upon the icy floor!"

"What icy floor? My house is warm! What have you seen? And why would it hurt you to see me? Haven't I been your friend, even if we have had today a small misunderstanding, whose fault I gladly claim?"

"I must go home now. I must go home to my man and my son. They need me. They will do a dance when they see me. I will keep my promise. I will give them berries and feed them cream."

Eliza crossed her arms over her chest. She looked straight at me a long time, then cocked her head.

"First come and look at my garden," she said.

"I will not come with you," I said. "I have looked through the bark and seen what is here."

"Ah, the bark," she said. "That little girl is always playing tricks. You were given a gift to twist the light and make you doubt. All you see through that bark is your own portion of sadness, Goody. Nothing more."

"What it showed me seemed no trick, or less a trick than all this fine world now behind you does. It's too early for plants such as these to be up!"

Eliza nodded. She smiled. She tossed her pretty hair, and the goose honked and the cow behind her lowed.

"Go, then, Goody. We will visit my gardens another day. Perhaps we will take a swim out into the water. You can swim, can't you? Sometimes Captain Jane comes to swim with me there, for she loves the water too and has also been granted the use of it."

"I will never visit your gardens. Or swim in your swamp."

Eliza's smile did not waver. In fact, it grew stronger. It grew stronger and she gave her shoulders a hearty shrug.

"Go on, then, my poor, pretty darling. I can see you still need it. Go home."

I hurried then away from her and that place as fast as my feet would allow me. Now, at every other step I took, the woods heaved into black and deep and drear. The air I moved through went from warm to cold then back again as if summer and winter were battling. I saw a great black wolf with bloody jaws when I took one step and a huge bird with a rotten fish speared on the end of its beak when I took another. I wished I could close my eyes to rub and clear them but didn't dare as there were roots and sharp branches all about. Whatever had been out on the water beyond Eliza's welcoming arms followed behind me. I felt sure of it. I could hear it coming, faster and faster. Faster and faster I ran.

Still, the farther away from Eliza's gardens I got, the better I felt, and by the time I reached her house, just that moment bathed in light from the late afternoon, I felt silly for having taken fright. As a girl I had seen spirits and goblins aplenty. I was not alone in this. When she was young, my mother fell into a hole filled, my father told me, with brilliant-hued birds. A hole in the ground. She told her parents what had happened and that the birds had been kind but now she had climbed out, now she was safe. Her parents hugged her and held her close, but when soon after creditors came calling, and they were forced to flee and find their fortune elsewhere, they said my mother was a slave to the Devil and left her behind with only a few sundries and a chest of cloth too bright to be sold in the gray towns of our coast. Once I asked my mother to tell me about the hole and the birds it was filled with, but she raised her large finger and wagged it before me, then begged God's forgiveness and cuffed me hard across the face. I did not speak to her of such things after that and standing outside Eliza's sturdy stone house in the sunlight, I found it was possible to imagine there were no such things, not even those I had just seen. What had I seen? I spoke sometimes in the night to my son about dead things that shivered and twisted in my head. Perhaps these were things like that. I had told him once, with my voice raised, about the hole filled with birds, but of course I could not be sure he understood me.

Thinking of my son and my mother and her ideas about dreams and the devils that hid in them, and about my wedding day, when she had locked me in my room while she went to get my man so that we might be married, made me weary, and I had the idea to step inside the stone house and rest a little on my borrowed bed or sit down again on the moss beneath the sugar maple, but at that moment the wind rose, the sun vanished, and the pigs began to squeal loudly in their pen. As I watched, first a great brown sow with black ears stood up on her hind legs, and then another, smaller pink one did the same. They stood staring out at me then turned slowly to face each other and embraced.

"On a day as strange as this, a trick as fine as that deserves reward," I said. I went around to the far side of the house and pulled open the doors of the root cellar. Thinking I would fetch them some fine treat from Eliza's rich stores, I went quickly down the steps, slipping a little on the moss. But the shallow cellar was not as it had been when I had sat in it with Eliza. There was no sweet marjoram and sage hanging from its rafters, no brine of egg or bean, no rack of apple or pear, only a mess of husks and bones, which lay cracked and scattered all about. The chest was there but it was shut tight and I did not try to open it. The barrel was there too. It took me a moment to understand what lay now upon it. There was no long goose quill this time. There was just a little feather, the very one tinged fiery orange I had been given by the robin and had had stolen by the crow. Its little end had been sharpened to a point and darkened as if it had been dipped. Beside it, on the barrel board, lay a small piece of dried skin upon whose hazed and hairy surface was the blotch I had made when I tried to write my name.

"Is this treat enough?" I said to the sow with black ears when I had climbed the cellar steps and was again outside. She shouldered her smaller fellow aside, gave the little piece of skin a sniff, then lifted up her mouth, took it delicately with her tongue, and ate it. She grunted after she had chewed and swallowed, then looked past my shoulder. Following her gaze, first with my eyes, then with my feet, I came to the border between Eliza's yard and the heavy tree trunks and found my shoes. They were filled with early flowers. Amidst the whites and yellows lay a plug of the same dark root that Captain Jane had fed me on my first journey to Eliza's, so I knew who had put them there. I emptied the shoes and put the plug in my pocket. My feet had swollen and I feared I would no longer fit into them. It took me some while, but soon I had them on and laced neatly and felt sure they would see me home.

CHAPTER 15

FOR MANY steps it seemed like my good shoes were leading me in the right direction. My man was skilled with leather and had crafted them from supple kid flank. They were sturdy of sole and had long since stopped chafing me. My son had a pair to match, though of course his were softer and smaller. The day before I had left to pick berries, he had worn them into the middle of a muddy puddle, put his arms over his head, and done a dance. He had put his arms down and come over and stood before me upon the completion of his messy dance and I had shaken him so hard that he had wailed. After I had counted to ten, I picked him up and dried his tears, then wiped at his pants and cleaned his shoes. When I saw that he would not stop crying, I told him I would weave a bit of colored cloth into his laces. Wouldn't that be nice? I had vermilion, I told him, magenta, shredded indigo.

"These have been torn special for you by your grandmother!" I said. This made him wail even louder so I kissed him and told him that they weren't his grandmother's colors, though they were, and had him choose one color for each of his shoes. He pointed at magenta for the left and indigo for the right, and I told him that was just the choice I would have made, that those colors went beautifully with the seashell favor he wore always around his leg. My man came in while I worked, looked at my son, then at me and all the colors, shook his head, muttered his prayer, ate something, then walked out again. As soon as he was gone, my son went and sat by the glass bottle of flowers I kept on the table when the weather warmed. He had never cared much to look at the flowers that drooped and wilted in the dim air of our little house but loved to sit with his feet dangling from his chair and gaze and gaze at the stalks in their browning water. Sometimes, as on that day, I would sit with him and tell him stories. In the bottle was a watery country. He and I lived in this country together and we were happy there but were too shy to show ourselves to the giants who peered in at us. We were little eels and so happy. My son took the bottle and turned it around, hoping, I supposed, to spot the little eels at play in the brackish water. "Stop now," I said. "You will never see them. They are not really there." But he kept turning the bottle and putting his face ever closer, then he looked at me and back at the bottle and pointed. And it did seem to me when I gazed close that I saw something in the middle of the stalks, bits of color wearing watery shoes.

I thought of all this while I strode away from Eliza's house and it struck me, taken entire and after all I had seen or not seen, as a good thing to think of, that quiet work on those laces and looking into the murky water with my son. Still, even if some of it was good, my memory of that day before I went to find berries was also a twisty thing. An hour after I had given him his cleaned and prettied shoes, my son was dancing in the mud again and this time waving the bottle of faded flowers above his head. "Those *are* your grandmother's colors and you look just like her, dancing and waggling your arms around," I told him. When my man came home and found him howling in his muddy shoes, it was my turn to get a scolding.

Evening found me walking far from the good road. I had taken up a stick and though at first I had used it for walking, I had long since left off leaning on it and now dragged it behind me, leaving a ragged line, like the ones I had made on Eliza's paper, through the leaves and dirt. I made my line past leaning oaks and lonely wood lilies, many of them already dried and dead, then up a slippery trace that took me, as darkness fell, through a thicket of damp, branchless birches, where in a small opening in the ghostly trunks I came upon a well.

It was lipped in mossy stone and wore the tattered remnants of a roof. As I was thirsty from all my walking, I thought I might steal a drink from its depths but though there was rope, no cup or bucket hung from its end. Yet even had there been a bucket I would not have drunk from those waters, as the smell that came up from the well made me shudder to my bones. I had smelled a fouled well before. If this wasn't death, it was death's dear cousin, and had my lips been three times as dry I'd never have let them touch it. The surface of the water resembled old porridge. Or a slurry of soiled ice. If my stick had been long enough I could have written upon it, but what would I have said? Perhaps I would have tried—and this time succeeded—to make my name again. When I looked up, there was an old woman standing on the other side of the well. She was aged and bent and staring down at the water as I had been. I saw behind her the opening of a path that dropped down a slope into the trees and thought she must have crept up from there.

It took me a moment to stop being startled and realize I had met her before. She had come one morning to our door selling rags and trinkets. My man had not stopped in his work in our field to see her off, so it was left to me. I told her we had no need of her wares and little to offer even if we had. She pulled prettier things then from the deepest reaches of the sack, which I might have looked at carefully and asked to hold had my man not been at hand and watching even as he fought the stony earth. Seeing her here in the woods, I grew excited, for I knew that as a tinker and traveler of lonely roads, she must know the way out of the trees.

"Greetings, mistress!" I said.

She looked, in the slant of what was left of the day's light, like a figure cut from fine parchment, and indeed she seemed to crinkle when she heard me. She wore a necklace of dried leaves and flowers that sounded when she placed her hands on the well's edge and lifted up her head. Even straightened, she seemed bent almost double, as if by special corset, and her hair hung in fatty clumps from a blotched, brown skull. I saw a tooth in her mouth when she called out a kind of whispery greeting, but only one, and it was black. The eyes she peered up at me with were wet with brine and yellow as mustard plucked and spat on and mashed in a gourd. Her wrists were thin, and wrapped around one of them was a length of dark and tattered string.

"I am lost from my road, mistress," I said. "Will you set me on my right way? You have been to my house and we have met before."

"Lost from your road, you say?" she said.

"I am come from Eliza's, across the wood." I pointed off into the dead birches behind me as if I hadn't been walking for such a while and what I was pointing at was only over the rise I had come down.

"Then you are just the one. Yes, just the one," she said. She reared back a little as she said this and continued to look at me through the cake of age on her eyes.

"The one for what, mistress?"

She leaned forward again, narrowed her gaze. "I have had things stolen and you are come from Eliza's and so can help me."

"Stolen! Of course I will help you if I can."

105

"I am searching for them. I slept and woke and saw that I had dug into my sleep too deeply, for first one, then the other was gone. Now I have come out to see where they can be."

"Were they lost in these trees?"

"They weren't lost—they were stolen!"

"I meant only that they were lost from you. It is I who am lost. Or turned about. We have met before, don't you remember? At my house? I have been lost and stayed on too long at Eliza's and must now go home."

"Home?" she said. "That's not what I lost."

She appeared for a moment to grow confused. Her breathing came harder and louder and she lifted up one of the hooked hands I remembered now from her visit to my house and touched it against the chain of leaves and flowers around her neck. She said something I could not hear and I asked her to say it again but more loudly. She did this and I heard her this time but she spoke in a language I did not know and did not like, for it sounded as though she were speaking through a long, hollow reed, or letting the words drip from her nose.

I asked her if she had come from far away, as I knew others living like her in the woods had, and if she had grown up speaking the tongue she had just used or if she had learned it in her later years, perhaps from a traveler like herself. Instead of answering, she pointed down into the well, cleared her throat, and said, "I'd like a drink."

"But there is no bucket."

"No bucket?"

"And I fear the water is fouled."

"Smells sweet to me," she said. "But you're right. There is no bucket. I'd forgotten that. If you want to drink from this well, you have to bring your own."

"Do you sometimes bring a bucket?"

"I was Eliza once."

"Beg pardon?"

"I said to you, good child, that I was Eliza once."

A smile grew on her crooked face and then a frown and her hand dropped again to hang at her side like its fellow.

"Your name is Eliza, mistress?" I said.

"I have had first one thing and then another stolen and you can help me," she said.

"Will you show me my path? For I must not delay. I went to pick berries for my man and my son, after we spoke at my house, and became lost," I said.

"Lost?" she said.

"Yes," I said.

"Then your path, Eliza, lies down and down and down this hill."

"I am not Eliza, mistress. I am come from Eliza, who lives in a stone cottage in the woods some way from here. Do you mean down the hill behind you? Or back the way I have come?"

"Yes, Eliza," she said.

My father spoke once to me of the fools who serve kings and queens. He spoke of them long after the juggler had played his angel/devil trick on our rain barrel, though I thought as he spoke that it must have been on his mind. He told me that for all their flips and cartwheels, japes and juggling, it was their tricks of the tongue that led you to laugh until you could not breathe and perhaps began to grow tight in your chest and sometimes even died. I said to my father that I did not believe you could die of a laugh and he looked over at me and said, "Poor daughter, you can die of nearly anything." I asked him if he could tell me some of what they had said, these jesters, and he told me he had only heard of them in stories and did not know just what they might have said, only that it was all twists and riddles and wouldn't it be grand to stand off in a corner and, while the king or queen took their entertainment, just wait there quietly, with nowhere else to be and no one to trouble you, and listen? What a journey that would be, to hear such jokes and stories!

That was the end of our talking that day and, until the very end, perhaps any other, and soon after he had left on his own journey and was in his grave.

"I remember you, young farmer's wife, who sharped a blade and stole a life," said the old woman and as she said it she began waving her arms beside her as if they were tentacles and we were in a tide pool or at the bottom of the sea. "So I will take you through the trees, I will take you through the ground,

I will take you through air and water, Eliza, I will take you all around."

"Call me Goody, if you like. I just want to go home, mistress," I said.

"Yes, go home," she said, letting her old arms fall.

"Will you show me the way?"

"I've dropped something in this well."

"I thought it was thirst brought you to this place."

"I am always thirsty for what's in this well."

"What's in this well? I thought it was things stolen that were troubling you."

"Dropped and stolen both."

She beckoned. I came around and stood beside her.

"Fetch it for me."

"Fetch what, mistress? What have you gone and dropped into this gray water that smells like death?"

"Bring it to me and you shall see," she said.

"But what is it?"

"You'll know it. I know you will."

She stretched out a long, bent finger. "There it is! Can't you see it? There at the very bottom."

"What is it?" I said. I leaned over the edge to look. The fouled water gave back no reflection. She shoved me in.

CHAPTER 16

"SWIM, NOW, my darling, swim, swim." It was my mother who first took me to the shore, who hitched up her skirts and mine then waded out into the water with me, who held me in her strong arms before she let me go. My father would sit and watch in the grassy sand or rove about and hunt for clams like his mother before him. He could not swim. Nor could my mother but she was not afraid, not of water, not of waves, not of currents that could make you drown. "Swim now, child, and it's never you will need saving." Soon I could swim like a silvery fish. I swam deep. I swam far. I could have lived, and very well it seems to me, in a water vase. As soon, though, as my mother saw I could do it she dragged me out by my ear because I didn't come back to her quickly enough and was yelling and splashing in a manner she found unseemly. I said it was only that I was so very happy. She said that happy meant less than nothing in the house of the Lord and never took me down to the water again. But my father did. By moonlight in the warm months he would tap my shoulder when my mother growled deep in the caves of her dreams. We walked out through whispery warm breezes and forests of feathery water grasses so that I could swim in the milky dark. My father spoke but little as we walked for he did not like, he said, to interrupt the songs of the frogs and crickets. He would not come into the water but sat always near me where I swam. Swam and swam. Until my mother followed us out one night with her switch.

"Swim now, Eliza," cried the old woman as I splashed and gasped and cursed, for the water she had shoved me into was not just foul, it was fearsome cold and gooped thick with the gray muck I had seen from above. It fell across my face and spilled in splotchy clumps from my arms when I lifted them. I tried to grab for the rope but the old woman yanked it from my reach. She told me it would be waiting when my errand was done. There was no other way up. I pounded at the water around me. I called the old woman a dog's tongue and a tart's dead daughter for the trick she had played. She said she was better and worse than either of those things, much better and much worse. I could not see her face for water was dripping over my eyes and the dim light of the sky was behind her but I could feel her black-tooth smile. "I'll see you down the hill, my darling," she said. As she spoke she tore a leaf from her necklace and let it drop. Back and forth it fell no more quickly than a fleck of down. When that one had almost touched the water, she let another go. More leaves fell to lie upon the heavy surface, and she said, "Remember your promise, given free, remember your promise, fetch it for me." I heard these words and watched the leaves in the shaft of the well and floating on the water's gray skin. I felt calmer as I watched and listened and soon stopped my thrashing and thought no more of calling names. Had I said I would help her? It seemed to me I had. I took a breath, then took another and plunged.

Of course, I had never traveled to the bottom of a well before nor watched one dug, so I could not know if it was strange that the tunnel dropped straight only a short while before curving into a slope. Nor did I know if it was strange that this well was darker near its surface than in its deeps, but darker above than below it was. As I descended, the water cleared itself of its muck and I began to see smooth stones and coins and bits of bone and teeth and mossy tokens of all kinds caught along its sloping floor. Some of these things I touched at but none of them looked like something the old woman would have missed, so deeper I went. I would have stayed down there and further fouled the well if I had not come at last to a kind of watery chamber lit by a crack above.

My kicking and paddling had set clouds of muck and slime to swirling and tokens from the slope to tumbling. Still, even through the murk and debris, I could see what the old woman had sent me down to fetch, for it glowed its own silver and I knew it, as she had said I would. It was lodged on a nest of more bits and bones. It was smooth and shaped like an egg. My hand went out. An extra chill met my fingers. As if they had found a deeper well within the well.

When I reached the surface again, the rope was waiting for me. I slipped what I'd fetched into the pocket of my dress and, hand over hand, shoes fighting for purchase on the slimy stone, dropping clods and clumps as I went, climbed slowly out. I lay chilled and panting in my sodden skirts on the rough ground of the clearing for what seemed like an age until I remembered the root I'd found with my shoes. It lay beneath the old woman's prize in my pocket. I did not like to think of that cold thing lying atop it but pulled it out and put it in my mouth anyway. Chewing it, even sogged as it was, stopped my shivering and my panting. I was soon neither warm nor cold and a smile crept onto my lips. By and by, I thought of the old woman's words about going down the hill when I had completed my errand. So I rose and wrung out my hair and dress and went to the place where I had first seen her peering off into the trees. There I found a path and followed it.

CHAPTER 17

THE PATH was well worn, and though it twisted I made good progress and thought to myself that perhaps despite her trick, the old woman with her leaves and rhymes had set me on the right way, some clear road through the wood that would lead me—once she had claimed the prize that bulged now in the pocket of my dress—in an hour or three to my man and my son. They would run out the door to greet me and we would link hands and turn a happy circle and what an ending to my tale it would be. I would be dry by the time I reached them and would not have to squish and squelch as I did now, though such loud sounds as my shoes were making would have pleased my son. His was always a quiet kind of laughing— not the sort it seemed you could die from—but I watched him closely nonetheless and sometimes took him in my lap and held him tight if it went on too long. Even if silence was all that came out of his mouth when he had finished, the laughing lent his cheeks a pretty bloom.

It was while I was squishing and squelching and pleasing myself with such thoughts that I came after a time of walking to a lightless cottage. Fat, syrupy drops had begun to drip from the sky and the plug of root I chewed was nearly spent and my chill was returning and though I did not like the look of this place I went as straight toward it as I had to the depths of the well. There were holes in its thatch, and its chimney sat askew, and I thought this cottage must be empty of all save rats and foxes, dust and spiders, ash and mice. But the cottage was not empty. When I knocked, a familiar voice rang out. "Come in, my love, come in!"

She was sitting in a chair by a dead hearth. She was no longer wearing the necklace of leaves and flowers and had wrapped a blanket tight around her.

"Come and warm your wet bones," she said.

She pointed at an empty chair. I went to it and sat. The old woman opened her mouth as I was doing so and I caught a glimpse of the tooth I'd seen before. I thought now that perhaps it had company, that I could see another rough bit of black at the back of her mouth, perhaps two. Seeing the black back of her mouth made me wish I had the child's bark again and could look through it and see if it showed better or worse what was before me.

"There, now, you're settled, Eliza," she said.

"Thank you, mistress," I said. The old woman turned and looked at the dead fireplace. She leaned forward and nodded

115

contentedly. A heavy kettle with a hole in its side sat unevenly on a pile of ash.

"Have you no fire? No light?" I said. I shivered as I said this for I had spat what was left of the root on the ground before entering and there was a draft coming down the chimney as well as drops of rain.

She turned and looked at me, cocked her head.

"But there is fire enough here to burn down a barn and all is brightly lit. Can't you see it?"

I shook my head. The woman frowned and lifted her arms. She groped at the piece of old string on her wrist as if reassuring herself it was still there. She shut her eyes and moved her lips and whispered more words in what seemed like the same strange language she had used before.

"Can you see it now? Can you feel the fine fire and hear the kettle sing?"

"I can't, mistress. I'm sorry."

The old woman opened her eyes and shrugged. "Come and sit a little closer to me, that's a good girl."

"I am not Eliza," I said.

"Of course you're not, Goody, and nor am I. Eliza lives in her sweet stone cottage and tends her grand garden and writes her tale and waits on the pleasure of her master and the master of us all. We do not forget. We never do. How could we? Why should we? But never mind that now, come closer. With my old ears I can't hear you when you speak as well as I might."

I did not much like to do it but pulled my chair a little closer to hers.

"Closer," she said.

I moved my chair again.

"Still closer," she said.

I hesitated but could not seem to do anything but move it one last time.

We sat now almost knee to knee. There was a smell of old wet cloth, of fouled water, of folds and flaps left to pile too deeply. So closely did her blanket and my skirt mingle near the floor and her feet and my shoes scrape and bump that I could not say if the smells came from me or from her. A smile that seemed larger by far than her wrinkled face could accommodate had curled over her lips when I sat and now something like a tongue but long and dark came out and dabbed up and down at them. Her eyelids gave a flutter when this thing had finished its work and she sighed.

"Give it to me now, that's a good girl," she said.

Her hand floated up and hung in the air between us. My old granny's hands had been curled and blotched like this one. I had often held them after her work with the clams or as she sat dozing in her chair before my mother took her away. I had pressed my cheek to them. Rubbed them with chopped mint and oil. The old woman's gaze was fixed on my skirt pocket. If her eyes blinked, I did not see it.

"Give it to me," she said with shaking arm now full out-stretched.

I would have given it to her. For in her voice I felt the waters of the well and the dropped leaves swirling all around me. This was the path I had chosen; I could see that now. She would have her prize and I would wander away into the deepest part of the woods and wear old berries for my eyes. Or climb up her chimney or crawl into her empty kettle. Or jump back into the well and drown. But even as I moved my hand toward my pocket, Captain Jane, dressed in her wolf-skin cloak, burst through the front door, swept into the room, took two quick steps toward us, and smacked the old woman's hand away from me. She then smacked the old woman, knocked her straight off her chair. I gasped and stood, thinking to go to the old woman's aid, but instead of lying in a heap where she had hit, the old woman gave an angry cry, half rose, and, with a speed that startled me, scuttled off to a corner of the room. There she turned, crouched, gathered her blanket around her, and glared at us. As I watched, the glare fell away and a sly look replaced it. She held out her arms. She was naked under the blanket.

"Come and give us a kiss, young darling," she said. "And give me what you fetched. It will save you years of trouble if you do. Years of peril and pain. Did you read what I wrote on the leaves I dropped around you? I need no quill of goose's tail. I need no paper. I need no nail. I scratch my meaning with the tooth of a ferret on leaves as old as stones. You've been warned. Give me what you have. Stand away from that thief or she will steal it from you. She means to have everything and quick."

"This is Captain Jane, who helps those lost in the wood!" I said.

"I know her and call her thief," said the old woman. "Traitor and thief to those who have helped her in the past. Make her give me back my cloak. Make her give back all she has stolen from me. Come now, deary, do not fear, take it now and bring it here."

Her voice, which had been high and thin, had dropped as she spoke, even more than it had when I had frolicked in fury in the water below her, as if it were emerging from a hole much deeper than a well, and, hearing, I began to turn toward Captain Jane, to lift my hands, to reach for the cloak.

"Take it now, my pretty cow," said the old woman, and my hands, seeking purchase, caressed the smooth, soft fur until Captain Jane struck them down.

"Follow me," she said, moving toward the door. "Don't listen to her and follow close."

Her voice was not so deep but it was fierce and loud. I dropped my hands and took one last look at the old woman— who, still crouching, had closed her eyes and lifted her own hooked hands high in the air and begun to speak in her strange language—then stepped quickly away from her and out the door.

As soon as I had drawn even with Captain Jane I started to speak. But she cut me short.

"Not now, love," she said. "Not here."

CHAPTER 18

IT WAS more than an hour of rude walking through the night before Captain Jane would speak to me at all and then only to instruct me sharply not to lag. Every minute or so she would cast a glance over her shoulder into the trees behind us and twice she made me stop and crouch silently on the forest floor. The second time she did this she unclasped her cloak and covered us with it. I could hardly breathe under the heavy fur and had to grip her forearm to keep my focus and not be smothered. If she felt my nails, which dug deeply, she gave no sign.

"She is desperate and at the end of her strength and has called out her greatest servants to try and catch us," she whispered. "The greatest servants she has left to her. It's I who wear this sweet black blanket now, so the wolves won't bother us. And count your blessings it's not her who calls the swarm!"

"The one that chased that poor man?"

"There are no poor men. Not even among the wretches."

"He only tried to help, to tell me to take my berries and run away home."

"I know that, dear. He wants us clear of the woods. He wants all of us gone."

"So you chased him away. For having tried to help me."

"Not I."

"Then who?"

Instead of answering the question, Captain Jane whispered, "Do you still have it? The thing that sat blobbed and fat in your pocket and that your fingers were reaching for when I came in. The thing that old teacup in her broken cottage is spending her last strength to get."

I felt at my pocket. "Yes," I said. "If she commands all these great servants, then why didn't she just take it from me?"

"Because it must be freely given."

"I did not feel free when I sat before her, nor when I swam in that foul water. I felt as if I was doing what I had been told."

"Speak more quietly. That means nothing. Those were only small tricks. Drops of grease to ease the turning of your mind. You told her you would help her."

"How do you know that?"

"Because I have been watching and listening, deary, and a good thing too."

Captain Jane growled these last words, then put her finger to her lips, pulled the cloak off of us both, and bade me follow. Told me to fly on my feet, now, if I didn't want to be supper for

Granny Someone, for that was who I had been fetching things for, that was whose house I had been in. Off in the near distance I thought I heard a heavy crashing. It was full dark and the way was tangled, but I had on my sturdy shoes and, damp as I still was, I ran. Faster than I had ever moved my feet. Once, a brood cow had chased me for coming too close to her calf, and there were some who saw me that day who said they had never seen anyone move faster. But that night in the wood, no matter how quickly I kicked my feet, I couldn't close the distance between me and Captain Jane. She ran like she was being sucked along a string of lightning, and if she hadn't finally stopped, I know I would have lost her and gone running forever through the dark or been swept up in the claws of our pursuer. But stop Captain Jane did, and suddenly enough that I almost missed her and her wolf cloak in the dark. I was so winded that I bent straight over and retched. Captain Jane did not breathe heavily at all. Her eyes were fixed on the path behind us. I regained my breath, stood up straight.

"Why has it stopped?" I asked.

"It cannot visit here. Its chase is done."

"Here where? Where is this? Where are we?"

I spoke too loudly in my fresh confusion. Dark maple and tangled mulberry surrounded us and there was a chill of mist to make further misery of my damp clothing.

"In my house. Where even Granny Someone's servants may not come."

"But who is she?"

"Have you never heard of her before tonight?"

I told her I had heard that name spoken more than once at Eliza's but thought she must be some old, kind friend who came with presents. Now, though, I did not like the name for I had seen the waking part of what answered to it.

"She is the greatest of us who live in the woods."

"Are there more of you I have not met?"

"There is only one of me, deary!"

Captain Jane winked, then reached into her small bag and pulled a nutshell from it and out of the nutshell she scraped a paste that she rubbed into the raw place where I had squeezed her arm. As she rubbed, a wolf howled. It was not far away. Captain Jane put away her nutshell and pulled tight the edges of her cloak. It shone somehow in the dark light and I thought for a moment the howl had come straight from it.

"So is it hers, this cloak you wear that kept us safe from the spirit?"

She shrugged as if I had asked about a stolen apple or a handful of hay gone missing from a barn.

"Granny Someone has a piece of string on her wrist like you do."

She slipped a long, thick finger under her own piece and pulled hard on it as if to show me how sturdy it was.

"They don't keep their color forever, though. This used to be near crimson. It was so bold you might have thought I'd cut

123

a canal around my wrist. You could have splashed in it and swum. Round and round and round and done!"

"You're as mad as she is."

"Perhaps I am."

"Are we safe now?"

"Never. Not in these woods. And not even with this cloak that makes the wolves call out to me with such love. But I do know Granny Someone's spirits will not trouble us anymore this night."

"Who says Granny Someone's servants may not come here?"

"Why, the lord of this wood and many a land beyond, love."

"Who is this lord?"

"Red Boy, love."

"Red Boy?"

I saw a quick red rippling in the trees, then fell and dreamed.

CHAPTER 19

I WAS back at my old house near the great, waving sea. My husband was at the shore with my son and had clambered out onto some rocks and was holding my son up in the air above deep water and playing at pretending to drop him. My son was crying. My son could speak and said he did not want to go down into the water this day. My husband saw me coming toward them. "Here is your mother, she will catch you, she always takes good care of you, she always keeps you safe," said my husband. "Catch him, Goody!" he called and let go. As my son fell, the water below him turned orange, then brown, then deepest, darkest red. I leaped to try and catch him and we both dropped through the cold, one after the other, and drowned.

"Come, love," said Captain Jane when I opened my eyes. I stood straight up.

"Is it still there?"

"You mean that precious thing in your pocket? I haven't

touched it. Nor would I without your leave. You spoke and fainted."

"Not that," I said, though I felt quickly at the front of my dress to be sure. "I saw something. Before I fell. Something in the woods. Like a length of red rope flying through the trees."

She raised her eyebrow and clicked her tongue. Looked at her forearm. If there had been nail marks there before, they were now gone. *I should pray,* I thought, for the dark was heavy all around, but when I bowed my head and pressed my hands together, my palms felt as if they had begun to burn.

"Not in this woods, deary," said Captain Jane.

"You are a witch," I said.

"I do not know that word. I am what Red Boy calls me. We are all what Red Boy has told us we are. Once Red Boy has bellowed in your ear you are his forever."

"Eliza too?"

"Eliza most of all."

"I saw no red boy at Eliza's house."

"How can you be sure?"

"You play at Change About."

She raised an eyebrow. She laughed and shrugged. "I've heard it called other things and called it other things myself."

"It's what Eliza calls it."

"Eliza has many notions, for now she writes her tale and has time for them. Has she taken you to her water to swim? She has

126

lovely waters. Change About, indeed! One is you, two is me, three is her, four is she!"

She gave a hop as she said each number. When she said *four*, she landed with a great bang on the leaf-covered ground.

"Your master is a boy?" I asked.

She laughed.

I thought of my son. My quiet, dirty, dancing little man. "I would not take my lessons from a boy."

"You say that now, love."

"He must be much greater than a child. A child is a tiny thing. What can a child do?"

"Red Boy is and does what he pleases. He can come and whisper truth about your tomorrow as he rides your heartstrings into the world. If you didn't know how to listen, you would think you were hearing the wind."

"I would know what I was hearing."

"Would you, now?"

"What does he look like?"

"What is your worst dream?"

"I think I saw him in Eliza's room, the little one at the end of the corridor, and standing on the water near Eliza's house. And he was here, near us, before I fell, just now."

"Oh, he *is* near us."

"I want to go home."

For I did want this as I stood there next to Captain Jane. I wanted it for having tried to get there so hard and failed. And

failed again. For having been down the well and into Granny
Someone's foyer. I wanted to go home more than anything else
in the world.

"I know, deary," said Captain Jane. "And I can take you
there. After all, we must make use of it. For it is mine now. This
wondrous thing. The cloak I wear is not my only new treasure.
Come and see."

As she spoke, she led me a few steps through the trees to
what I took at first for a lidless chest then saw as we stepped
closer was something else.

"It is a fine boat, isn't it?" said Captain Jane. "I tried it earlier when I fetched your shoes from where you had left them by
the stream."

"A boat?"

"I cannot leave these woods without one."

"That's a strange rule!"

"Rules are the way of the world! Did you never dance? Did
you never stomp your foot around a ring of fire? Which way do
you step? Which way do you stomp? How do you decide?"

She gave a light step, then a smart, hard stomp. Then she
clapped her hands and pointed again at the thing before us.

The boat resembled a high-walled cart without wheels. It
looked as though the softest wind would blow it on its side.

"A few fine tricks with her voice she may still know, but she
is too old and too weak and does not need this boat anymore,"
Captain Jane said, as if speaking to herself. "There was a time

you could not come within a mile of her house without disturbing her sleep and if she caught you it was terrible. She had me once, lured me deep into the trees when I was no older than you, then took me below the ground and kept me for many days in one of her dark caves. They lie below her house. Below the woods. Below the world. But she is so old now. There is no log left to fire her furnace. You saw how I was able to strike her! To make her fall off her chair and run from me. Even in her own parlor. Still, her charms may be failing her, and she cannot weave a glamour for anyone with eyes, but if you had given her what she asked for she would have found fresh strength, then killed you and come for me and found more."

I pressed at the thing in my pocket. It was like a peeled egg, cooked then kept in the chill of a brine bucket.

"You *are* a thief," I said.

"Perhaps," she said. "And where's the fault? It's my time. Not hers. The cloak was easy. She left it lying outside her door as she slept. Right there on the ground! Almost as if she meant for me to have it. And she might have. There is always part of us admits we are done when the rest is not yet ready. This other lovely thing was not so easy, though. Not so easy at all!"

I did not respond. Only walked around and around the "lovely" thing. It was made of human skin and of human bones. I could see part of a face on its side. It had been stretched so much, its features could not be fully marked. There were bones thick and thin and skin lighter and darker in its design.

"Have the skins of those you *helped* the other night gone into this?" I said. "Perhaps the ones I saw you with that night?"

Captain Jane's smile fell from her face. She stepped closer to me than I liked. "This boat is old, dear. Its skins were stretched long ago and not by me nor any now in these trees. I helped those souls you saw with me. They made it away with Captain Jane's help, *my* help, just like you did!"

Seeing I had pushed at her harder than I should, I told her I was sorry for having doubted, to which she muttered something I couldn't hear. As we stood there, and as the night crept forward, a thought dressed as a memory came to me.

CHAPTER 20

THE HOUSE of my childhood and early marriage by the sea sat a
league from the town I have already mentioned more than once,
one built fast along the shore. It was a large and ever-growing
town with prosperous shops and fine men and elegant women
to walk its streets and keep its best houses and offer each other
an evening smile or blessing. This was the town my mother
had grown up in and the town in which she had been left behind. My father, who came from farther along the coast, did not
like the town nearly as much as my mother still did and when
she was walking its streets and peering into the windows of the
fine shops she had once frequented with her parents, my father
would walk me down by the water where the ships sat snug in
their moorings. Some of these ships were small and made for
fishing in shallow waters and some were large and had come
across the ocean with their cargo of all kinds. My father liked to
smoke his clay pipe and watch the ships. Sometimes he spoke
with the sailors who climbed down off of them.

On one of the days we came to town, my father assumed I would follow off after my mother and my mother assumed I would wander off after my father and I did neither. Instead, I chased seabirds and stole an oatcake then found my way to a small square, where a woman was languishing in the stocks. There were words written on the stocks but I could not read them. The fun was over and there was no one else around. The woman's eyes were closed and she was all but naked. Her hair had been shorn close and there was blood on her head where the skin had been scraped. I skipped up close to her and touched at her short hair and when I did, her eyes came open and she snarled. I have not yet forgotten that snarl. Nor those eyes. They were green as a mallard's plumes. When the snarl was finished, she shut them again.

I backed away from her then and chewed at my stolen oatcake and saw that the sun was growing weary. The woman was breathing loudly. Breathing and sighing. The air of the square went into her lungs loudly and came loudly out again. I tried to hear if I was breathing loudly too but couldn't. I wondered if her breathing was robbing my breathing of its own sound. Then I began to wonder if her breathing was robbing me of my breath, as if each time she inhaled, she was sucking away what was meant for my lungs. I was thinking this and starting to feel my chest grow tighter when I heard a heavy noise of swooping above the rooftops and stopped my thoughts of breathing and hid behind a sailor's cart. It was then I saw the boat, though of course I did not know what to call it. It floated down out of the darkling sky and bobbed a minute before the woman. A hand came out of the boat and touched the woman on her cheek. Then the hand went back into the boat and the boat lifted away. I followed it with my eyes until it became but a fleck in the sea of the sky. When I looked down again, the woman sagged in the stocks and her loud breathing had stopped. The shadows had grown long. I forgot which way I had come and ran off down streets that soon became unfamiliar. At the very moment my tears began to fall, a man with golden curls came up beside me. After we had walked a few steps together, he gently took my hand.

He was young and handsome and he asked me was I lost and I said I was and so he took me to his fine house and there, with a perfumed handkerchief, wiped the tears from my cheeks and the crumbs of oatcake from my mouth. He gave me hot milk and sugared biscuits and dandled me on his knee. He sang to me with a voice so pure I thought he must be hiding secret wings. I grew drowsy in the heat and he smiled at me and said he would make me up a cozy bed. He set me on a pillowed bench and I drowsed and when I woke, I saw a staircase leading down had appeared in the middle of the floor. The young man was no longer there and I crept over to the mouth of the stairs. The staircase was narrow and dropped away into a darkness deeper than any root cellar's. Up out of that darkness came a song I can no longer recall.

It was a day of wonders and I was so warm now, when I had lately been so lost and scared, and weariness had settled on me like a weighty hand. At home I had my bed but it was mean and small. I took the first step down the narrow staircase. I took the second. I began the third, then thought, *Father will not know where I am.* It was a simple thought but strong. *I will go and find Father and tell him and he can tell Mother and then I will come back to sleep in my new bed.* So I turned around and went back into the light and left the fine house where candles burned everywhere in painted sconces and went out into the dark and wandered until I could wander no more and fell asleep in the doorway of a milliner's shop.

I do not know how my parents found me. I do know that I told them about the woman who had snarled at me and about the sky boat I had seen and how I had been scared, though not about the handsome man who had fed me sweets, for that had seemed one secret too many, one I must keep for myself. I also know that even as we walked along the road, my father was chased and caught and struck by my mother for having let this happen and that he wept for it among the geese and chickens when we had made it back to our home. It was a long time before my mother would allow me to go again to the town, though the unearthly echo of the handsome man's song stayed with me.

I told this tale to Captain Jane as we stood before the boat that she had stolen from Granny Someone.

"A bed for you beneath the floors!" she said when I had finished my speech.

"Yes. I haven't thought of it in a very long time."

"Now there's a story that might have had another ending. You have sight uncommon and that you do. It's seeing that saved your skin more than once. Seeing's not the gift I came to these woods with. I understand why Eliza thinks it is you are the one can save her and can carry a thing through to its end."

I started when Captain Jane said this, sharpened my gaze and looked hard at her, for I had thought only of myself and not of Eliza when it came to the question of saving.

"'Goody's the only one can save me,' Eliza said when I brought your shoes."

"Eliza knew you had brought me my shoes?"

"Of course she did."

"But she wanted me to stay!"

"That's also true. Truth has many different drawers and shelves."

I waited for Captain Jane to go on but instead of saying more she slid open a panel that was neatly built into the side of the boat, split the stretched face in two, then stepped in and made room for me to follow. The deck was a piece of leather above a latticework of bones. As we shifted our weight, it moaned beneath our feet. From inside the boat it was easy to see the stitch work used to sew it all so neat. Captain Jane closed her cloak around me so that it was only the upper half of my head poking out. I told her I was well warm enough as I was and tried to move away but she held me tight and said where we were going it would be colder by far and only wolf skin could keep us warm.

I said nothing then. She gave a bark and the boat began to move, first far faster and louder than I could bear across the forest floor, then up with the branches of ash and maple and oak whipping hard against us. Then higher still, where there was only the wind.

CHAPTER 21

UP WE sailed into the sky. And over the sea of the forest. And through the dark of the clear night. And beyond great tunnels of wind and straight through a banner of ice-filled clouds. When we came out the other side, we found ourselves in the snow of an early-spring storm. The earth lay smothered in its whiteness below. All about us the flakes fell softly. Captain Jane asked into my ear was I warm enough. The wolf cloak had turned white and my face was half frozen.

"I am," I said. I was.

"Then would you like to stay in this fine boat and travel a small way through this night with me? For I have a mercy to perform."

"A mercy?"

"A service of sorts. You'll see. The boat will take us to it and may tell me more of it as we go."

"Does the boat speak to you as well as fly?"

Captain Jane smiled but did not answer. I said that I did not well follow what she meant about mercies and could not parse her smile but that I would stay with her a little longer if only to ride through the air and skid along past moon and storm, for doing so was what I had always dreamed. This was what, I realized, I was dreaming when my father came to me the next time my mother was away after that night on the beach and said we were leaving. He had booked us passage. "Passage, daughter!" he said. We were going far from these shores and would stay away forever. And because he said that on such a grand voyage we must go gaily dressed and had nothing but our daily drab to wear, he teased open the lock on my mother's treasure chest and we stuffed scarlet into our seams, indigo into our sleeves, aqua into our ankles and shoes. We slipped then from the house taking only the bits of color and what we could carry, only what would serve. It was as we walked quickly and merrily away that he told me about queens and fools. He said we were going to a place where we could still see them. "Would you like that, daughter?" he had asked me.

"Yes, I would like it very much," I said, speaking to Captain Jane. As soon as I said it, the boat, which had paused in its flight, leaped forward, then curved right and cut a long arcing half-loop through the frozen skies. As we went our way Captain Jane sang or laughed or sometimes howled. For my own part I kept very quiet, as quiet as I have ever been, for there are things in this world that you think will never come to pass that will rob you of your voice for nothing but the joy of them when suddenly they do. I was so happy there in our riding, and so hushed in my happiness, that when the boat slowed and lowered, then came to a stop above the cobbled street in a town, it took me a long time to move or answer Captain Jane when she leaned away from me and asked me was I coming in with her on her errand or would I like to stay outside in the frosty cold.

"Where have we arrived?" I said.

"A street in a town whose name I do not know," she said.

"Have we come as far as the sea?" I asked with some wonder. For even cold as it was, now that we had stopped moving through the air, I could smell it, as if the waves were washing slowly over the cobbles and splashing on my shoes. There was tar in the air, tar and salt and brine.

"Distance means little to a boat of the air."

"You know a great deal about boats and their habits for one who has just come into possession of one."

"I have long enough studied the subject," she said. "It is not just roots and herbs that I know the uses of. Now, will you come with me through this door and into this house, or will you stay here?" She had leaped over the side of the boat and onto the street and was pointing in a direction I had not looked at a stout oak door set in the side of a grand house. The windows of the house, at least on its ground floor, were brightly lit.

"Where have you taken me?"

Instead of answering, Captain Jane clapped her hands, stepped forward, and pushed open the door.

I gave a sniff. It was the sea for sure. I thought we must be well close to the water, for even a smell as grand as the sea travels poorly through frosty air. I slid open the gate of skin and stepped out of the boat and when I did, it lifted up into the sky as if I had released it and was swallowed by the falling flakes, leaving me to look about myself at the darkened street, where the snow gathered in the cobbles, and where a young elm grew, and where light poured from the fine house before me. I stood gazing at it from the frozen street, but soon my teeth were chattering and the tips of my feet and fingers had begun to hurt, for the world of that night in my damp dress without Captain Jane's cloak around me was terrible cold.

It was indeed a large, fine house with candles lit in sconces that led along a wide, central foyer. My eyes lingered on many a lovely object set quivering by rich wax light as I followed Captain Jane's glittering wet tracks across its burnished floors. Presently I came to another oaken door, twin almost to the one that looked out on the cold world, only this one was painted red as the sun. I was breathing hard and my body ached and groaned as it warmed, but I could hear over the din of my own ears that someone inside the room behind the red door was singing. The latch was warm and turned easily, as had the latch on the door to Eliza's small room, and for the briefest of moments I felt sure—even as I knew now where I must be—it was her I would find lying cold and still and near heart-stopped as she stared at something when I stepped beyond. But we were far now from Eliza, and this door, unlike hers, which had creaked, opened without a sound onto the kingdom of my memories, the larder of my dreams.

Captain Jane was standing before him. He was holding a violin in one hand and its bow in the other. The chair he sat on was high-backed and fine. He must have long since crossed the border of his middle years but was still as nice and more to look upon as I remembered him. He had the same flaxen locks that curled low on his forehead and arched golden eyebrows. His festive linen blouse fit snugly and his breeches were purple and green. As he sang, his elegant lips moved more, and pleasantly so, than it might have seemed they needed to, like they had their own dance and business to arrange. It was a lullaby came from his lips. One I had sung often enough in my own house without ever asking myself where it had been learned, though he made the tune turn differently. "Hush, child...Don't cry...Sleep now...Don't die..." His voice was high and sweet and there were tears in his eyes and on his cheeks as he sang. He had held no violin in his hand when I had been his guest before but that was all that seemed different about him. He made a picture, in his beauty—for beauty plain and pure and simple it had been all those years before when I had looked upon him with my child's eyes and it still was—that I had rarely put a frame on since I had last been in his house. The little table by the pillowed bench stood in its place but now it was a bowl filled past its rim with spring berries that smiled with the will-o'-the-wisp reflection of the candles upon it. There was also, just inside the door, an ink-splattered desk I did not remember on which sat a mess of pages covered in dots and lines that I soon realized were musical notes. The pages were larger by some good measure than Eliza's and many were rolled and tied with string. Some pages had fallen to the floor. Others had been crumpled into balls and thrown about.

I stepped full into the room and Captain Jane turned to me and, before I could ask her how she had brought me to this place when I had barely left off speaking of it, shook her head and put a finger to her lips. So I understood that there was a glamour at work, one that had its limits, meaning that if the handsome singer couldn't see us, he could still hear us. Indeed, as I moved toward Captain Jane, I stepped over a ball of crumpled paper and came down on a poorly joined floor plank that squeaked softly. The handsome man, who had been singing now about babes and wells and breezes, stopped. Captain Jane looked at me.

"Sing on," she said, taking a step closer to the man so that she was now at easy arm's reach from him.

"That is a different voice than the one that has long spoken to me from the shadows," said the man.

"The shadows hold many voices," said Captain Jane.

"Yours is not the one I know."

"The world is full of change."

"The world has not changed for me in a long time," he said sadly.

"You chose that changeless place. Now play."

The man rubbed his nose, bit at his lips, bowed his head. Then he slid the violin under his chin, crooked his arm, and drew the bow once across its strings. I saw with a thrill when he did this that his fingernails were as black at their smooth edges as mine had been before Eliza scrubbed them. It was one note he played. But it was shaped like a curving crown and dipped deep in the glitter of sorrow. I have never since heard longer or lovelier. Often here I call it to mind. It always comes.

"I want to stop, I said that the last time, I need to stop," said the man, yanking the bow away from the strings.

"Play on," said Captain Jane.

"I do not wish to play any longer."

"Then sing on, for there is another here who will like the chance to ride the harp of your voice, for she heard it sung snug against her ear when she was small. She heard it but ran away. She heard it and didn't stay."

"Who is it?" said the man, flicking his eyes nervously about the room. I counted twenty candles burning all about him. They hung from the ceiling; they sat in sconces, dripping their wax onto the polished floor. "Is it a spirit you wish me to sing for?"

"I am no spirit," I said.

He flinched when I spoke.

"Sing now," said Captain Jane. "Sing for her. Sing for *them*. Comfort your little pigs."

"I only keep them for our bargain."

143

"What bargain?" I asked.

"Tell the other voice who has come to me these many years, if it's still her I must parley with, that I wish to stop."

"Oh, I think it's me now, not her," said Captain Jane. "And we are not just voices, as I believe you know."

At this she pursed her lips, leaned forward, and blew. The man gave out a sharp cry when the air touched him, as if the burst of breath had burned.

"But you won't stop, will you, my beauty? For you started long before your bargain was struck." She turned to me. "Do you think he will stop?"

I did not answer. In listening to them, my mind had been filled to its own rim with boats and sugared biscuits and the handsome man and hissing women and languages I could not speak.

"Take your price and go. Take them all at once, though some are not yet ready and may not serve."

"What does he mean that some are not yet ready?" I asked.

"Sing," said Captain Jane.

"What do you mean?" I said to the man.

"Answer her," said Captain Jane.

The man gave a smile and then a sob just as small.

"Have you ever seen a veal calf?" Captain Jane said to me. "Tell your guest grown tall and free what you mean."

"It was our bargain."

"Tell her!"

Instead of telling me, he brought bow and violin down to his lap and began to sing. His voice started small then grew grand. It was like a giant from one of my old grandmother's stories had entered the room. As his voice flooded the tunnels of my ears and flooded the room and went through the plaster of the ceiling and the plank of the floor, Captain Jane pointed at the pocket of my dress, then mimed that she would borrow a moment what was there. As soon as he started singing my thoughts had scuttled away from veal calves and pigs and back to his face and his voice and his violin and on to the memories of warmth and the soft bed he had promised me, so it was distractedly that I pulled it from my pocket and distractedly that I put it in her hand. Captain Jane beamed, tossed the egg-shaped thing up into the air, and caught it when it came down. She waited a moment until the singer's mouth was open wide, then winked and shoved what she held into the hole.

At once the man's singing stopped. He tried to speak, then seemed to choke. His face went dark, then pale. He gave a great gasp, then sucked hard at the air. Then he began to scream. And such a scream! It was louder than the song he had been singing. It was deeper than the well in which I had swum. It was wilder than the rushing of the wind and the swarming and howling I had heard in the woods. Captain Jane laughed when I stepped back and put my hands over my ears and again when I quickly took them off for they did nothing to dim the ever-rising sound.

"What have you given him? What did I give you?"

"You gave me a scream. One grown special in dark water, fed by word, dusted by night."

"A scream?"

"I am letting him warm it for us and show its worth. Let's see how very loud and lovely we can make him, shall we?"

Captain Jane reached down and pulled a piece of crumpled paper off the floor. She smoothed it, studied it carefully, then threw it aside and winked at me. "One is you," she said. She crooked her arms and snapped the fingers of both her hands. Immediately the handsome singer's scream leaped higher and sharper. "Two is me!" she cried and cocked her hip and slapped her leg and the scream became as rich as a cake brought away from the oven just before it begins to burn. "Three is her," she hissed and rolled her head slowly around and around and the scream became thin as gruel and weaker still when she started to stalk around him and leaned in at intervals to puff on his face and head.

"Did you know I used to play? I don't think I've told you that," she said to me as the quiet screaming continued. "Not half as well as this sweet marvel, but yes, oh yes, I did."

"Play?" I whispered.

"Anything I could put my hands on!" She stopped her circling and reached out and plucked at each of the violin's strings. Then she cupped the singer's chin with her fingers and brought her face close to his. "Four is she," she whispered and jerked at his face and the scream burst back loud. "Four is she!" she roared and jerked his face again and the scream grew louder still. Ever closer she brought her face to his as she jerked it back and forth until it seemed their lips might touch.

"This is the song for our woods, don't you think, dear Goody? You could wait a hundred years and not hear a song as fine as this!" she yelled.

"Make it stop," I pleaded.

"Do you wish it to stop?"

"Yes."

"Are you certain? This is just a beggar's portion of what he has to offer us. That's a grand scream in his throat, a mighty scream. I've never seen or dreamed its like. It could pull the walls in on us. It could bring the ceiling down on our heads."

I nodded sharply. Captain Jane rolled her eyes and shook her head as if to say she had expected more from me. She let go of his face, patted his cheek, took a short knife from her cloak, and stuck it in his neck.

As quickly as he had stopped singing, the man stopped screaming and in the new-struck silence the violin and bow slid off his lap and onto the floor.

"But what is this? Why have you made him scream and now murdered him? What has he done? He is beautiful and his singing and playing are beautiful. Is this your *mercy*?" I said.

"Is it indeed?" said Captain Jane. "Have you truly not grasped what we have before us, what you *had* before you? You may have some small gift of sight but it's true it needs focusing."

"I had a bit of bark—" I said.

"I know about your bark and how it helped you squint," Captain Jane cut in. "But there are other ways it can be done."

Quick as you like, she leaped behind me, brought her hands over my eyes, raised her elbows, flipped her palms outward, then opened a gap like a long, squashed diamond between her fingers for me to look through. Immediately what sat thrashing and grasping at his throat went from murdered angel to murdered fly or monkey, one grown human-size.

For a moment after Captain Jane snapped the mask of her fingers away from my face, his mouth stayed empty of all but his terrible moaning, and his skin sagged and spilled from his fine clothes as if it were Granny Someone's brother stuffed into a gentleman's costume, then my eyes cleared, or fogged, and he was beautiful again.

Captain Jane, seeing my expression, which I could feel had straightaway softened, spat and said, "You see well what's there or ought to be and I have helped you see better, but you don't think. I had taken you for sharper by far than that!" She now stepped alongside the handsome man and with one strong gesture shoved him and the chair he sat on over sideways. The back of his head hit the low table where long ago he had served me my biscuits as he fell. With a flourish, Captain Jane then pulled up a small carpet that had sat below the man's chair to reveal a trap in the floor.

"Open it now and tell me if you understand! You won't need

the tricks of my fingers to see what he has been keeping and fattening for our friend Granny Someone!"

With these words, I saw again the boat descending from the air, floating above the stocks, the hooded figure within. Blood was pulsing from the man's throat, pooling on the wood plank, spilling into the cracks. Written here in bloody ink was the other ending to the story I had told Captain Jane in the woods. I stepped forward, took the trap by its iron ring, and pulled. The door was lighter than it looked but still gave up a deep grinding when it rose. A narrow stair, smaller and steeper than I remembered, dropped away into darkness. Captain Jane came and crouched beside me.

"Go down if you wish to meet what he was making his songs for, your handsome lad, see what he sang and played to every night before climbing up to his bed, see what he offered Granny Someone in exchange for his gifts of youth and beauty."

Captain Jane nudged me.

"I have been on these stairs before. I did not follow them then and think I will not follow them now," I said.

"Then wait a moment and they will climb up. They are timid, though, as well they should be. The light, even soft as it is, will be too bright at first, for they have not looked upon it for many a day. I have been held below the ground. I have been kept in the dark to ripen, to grow sweet and soft. To be eaten up like them. I was blind for hours after I came free from Granny Someone, as those below are like to be."

"Were you held like they are? Below the floor and down the stairs?"

"Oh, not quite like them. I was beneath the woods and there were no stairs and the walls were wet earth. But I had visitors as they did. Mine was Granny Someone and her wolves and spirits, and they came to look at me, fresh to the forest as I was, and lick their lips. He would climb down sometimes and drop sweets in their mouths and hold their soft and pale hands."

"Did the boat tell you all this?"

Captain Jane smiled. The man had stopped moving, all but his lips, which trembled still. The ends of his fingers were now red, not black. The blood had spread and caught some of his crumpled pages and kissed at the edges of his violin. For a moment the blood pouring from the knife hole in his throat stopped and the scream I had fetched from the well slipped its way out along the blade. It came forward in a rush of blood, rolled slowly down his crimson front, over his velvet pant leg, and lay blotched and bloody on the sodden floor.

"Look now!" said Captain Jane. "I see something. Can you see it? Lean close! Something stirs!"

I brought my eyes back to the stair and peered down into the dark. It was like looking into wave-washed water that has been flushed with sand. Or into the far corners of a dream that has come to the end of its shaping and does not know what colors to conjure next for itself. As I watched, a fat pale hand appeared. It placed itself onto one of the lower steps. And then I saw a fat naked shoulder, and then another, and then a fat neck and then eyes, farther down, one pair after the other, peering weakly up into the light.

Captain Jane nudged me with her elbow. A sly look had come over her face. "Perhaps you would like to play with them," she said.

"Play with them?"

"Or pray for them!"

"I thought you said it couldn't be done."

"We're not in the woods here. You could pray for them in this house, deary, and pray for him . . ."

She nudged me again. I tried pressing my hands together and easy as that, they touched.

"Go on," said Captain Jane.

"I do not wish to pray," I said.

"Not even for those poor little bulbs and roots trapped down there in the dark?"

"Those are children."

"And so they are."

"Did Granny Someone tell him that day to come and find me? After she had ended that woman's trial in the stocks? Is that how he knew I was there?"

"Do you begin to understand?"

"And he would have done this to me?"

"Of course he would have. He almost did. He has done it many times."

"And she would have eaten me after?"

"And ground your bones or built a little boatlet of them and stopped your story long ago. Are you sure you don't want to see? I want to see! Let's go down together. Will you fetch me my knife, deary? Look at them!" I looked and thought of Eliza's pigs. I half expected the pale things, which were gathering in ever greater numbers at the bottom of the steps, to give a greasy oink or grunt meaningfully.

"So soft they are and no doubt sweet. This is how she was keeping up her strength even as I was stealing away her meals in the woods! Well, no more of these treats for her!"

She asked me again to fetch the knife. "It's just it's struck me that, now that you have seen what he meant to do to you, you might like to at least hold its handle a moment, even give it a twist."

I looked at her, then looked at the dead man and at the knife, which had come looser as the scream had pushed its way out.

"No. It's the scream I want, not the knife."

Captain Jane raised her eyebrows. "You want to taste that scream, do you?"

"I don't want to taste it, I want to shove it in his mouth again!"

Captain Jane gazed at me, sat down on the floor, flung back her head, and roared. "Now we see your spirit!" she said, wiping at her eyes and sitting up again. "But that scream won't work on him now that he's dead."

"Won't it?"

"It will only get stuck. And then we'll have to take him apart to fetch it. That's a different kind of diving, that is. Give the knife a good twist or take a teardrop from his cheek. I see there are several. Go on. A good tear can come in handy. There is much can be done with a tear."

I crawled close to the dead man. Captain Jane crawled with me. We stopped at the edge of the pooled blood. I reached out with my right hand and touched one of the tears that clung to his cheek. It stuck to my finger like a warm jelly at the fair and sat quivering when I held it up to the light. "Give it a moment," Captain Jane said. I watched it sag and spread and form itself around my fingertip. As I touched, gingerly, at its spongy wetness, Captain Jane scooped up the scream and slipped it into her cloak. Then she took my hand and inspected my finger. "That's a good one and well stuck," she said.

"I have tears of my own if I need them," I said.

And she said, "You can never have too many tears."

"Teach me how to make a mask of my fingers."

Captain Jane brought a hand up to her face, flipped the palm outward, made a gap between her second and third fingers, and looked through it at me.

"What do you see?" I said.

"I see that it's not yet time for such teaching."

"When will it be time?"

Captain Jane gave a chuckle. She looked at me another moment then dropped her hand.

"Who knows, young Goody, who knows?"

I stood and left the room then. I left without another look into the hole in the floor or at the dead man. I did turn to the table where he had once served biscuits to me, took up the bowl, and tipped most of its bright red berries into my pocket where the scream had been. The street was as empty as before. Captain Jane came up quickly behind me, leaving the door to the handsome man's house open to the cold.

"Did you fetch your bloody knife or leave it in his throat?"

I said this with what I thought must sound like a fine and proper snort, for I felt suddenly tired of her and her secrets and her endings to stories I had not asked to know. Whether Captain Jane heard my tone or not, she simply patted the side of her cloak. The boat, as if it had been waiting for our return, now dropped from the snowy reaches of the dark above to float before us again just a hand's height above the cobbles. Already Captain Jane, smiling brightly, was stepping toward it.

"There is nothing so fine in Red Boy's world as a boat!" she said.

"What does Red Boy have to do with it?"

"Everything!"

I stepped in beside her. The bone planks below us creaked and crackled as they settled under our weight.

"Does it speak to you even now, this boat? Does it tell you other awful stories? Will it tell you where to go next?"

"Of course it does. Or they do. It has more than one voice, for it was more than one skin! Can you not hear them when they speak? Of course you can't. If they have somewhere they think we should go, they will tell me. I think, though, that our work of mercies is done for this night." She patted a bit of sturdy thighbone, ran a fingernail gently through the sheen of ice covering a long, stretched length of hide.

"Now," she said. "Shall we let the neighborhood know what's lived hidden among them all this time?" She didn't wait for me to answer. The boat took us first to one window, which Captain Jane broke with a blow of her elbow, and then another. "Fire!" Captain Jane bellowed. "Murder!"

When lights began to appear in the windows of the houses around us and doors were flung open, we rose in a silent rush. The snowy dark pressed close and Captain Jane's cloak came back around me.

"They'll find him," I said, after we had flown in silence for some time.

"And them."

"So there's the mercy."

"Their being fished up from the dark? No, not that..."

"Then what?"

"Think."

I thought. We flew straight up, then shot forward and through a flock of geese. Captain Jane tried unsuccessfully to grab one as we passed.

"Killing him was the mercy, like it was for the woman in the stocks," I said. "And it was right. He was a prisoner of the gifts Granny Someone had given him. He would have kept on but said he wished to stop. His torture must have been great."

My thinking seemed to fill Captain Jane with pleasure. She patted my cheek with her blood-sticky hand and said, "True enough, my dear, that I had to do it. But killing that monster was no mercy; killing him was simple turn and turnabout. You heard him. He had made a promise to Granny Someone and was refusing to keep it any longer. And making a promise to Granny Someone and not keeping it cannot be allowed!"

"You speak as if you were Granny Someone."

"Not quite. Not yet. But soon, perhaps."

"Then it was a mercy to me," I said. "To ease a pain I'd long forgotten."

"We all have pains we've long forgotten. But you said yourself this wasn't one. You left his house when it was still possible to think he truly had a soft bed and more biscuits for you! If you couldn't find it after and that troubled you, it was because Granny Someone worked to keep it hid."

"Then what was the mercy?"

"I told you earlier that you see but don't think, and it will undo you, deary," she said. "The mercy *was* for the children, but not in the way you imagine. The mercy, my deary dear, was closing and concealing again that cellar trap, for that is what I did before I left. Don't worry; they'll be found, those piggies, yes. We've seen to that. But not straightaway."

"Why not straightaway? How can that be a mercy?"

Captain Jane leaned in so close then I could feel the roughness of her lips.

"Let them stay safe in there a little longer," she said. "There is no hurry. How could there be any hurry? Haven't you seen how very dark it is out here?"

CHAPTER 22

WE FLEW then in long silence. I saw the handsome singer's face appear before me as it had been when I was young and as it had been before it had had its throat stabbed open and as it had looked through the mask of Captain Jane's strong hands. I stretched out my finger and felt an extra thrill of cold where I'd harvested his tear. The knife had been small but had quickly done its work. One little hole in the right place and the life leaks out. No need for many. I saw too the long staircase and the little figures below and the darkness that had closed back upon them. But my mind kept going back to the singer, to his song and to his scream, which now seemed as like in my thoughts as well-made twins. Captain Jane poked me, and my eyes came open and I saw we had gone skidding up and out over the snow clouds. The moon hung fat near the horizon. Stars loitered in the blackness all about.

"I would like to go home now, please," I said. I spoke softly, but Captain Jane heard me for I felt the boat softly turn and she spoke. "It is fine that you want to go home and that you are going home. I might go home too if I could."

"But why can't you? If you wanted to. It seems you do what you want."

"I have already told you, deary. I am Red Boy's and could not go a fairy's inch without his proper leave."

"What of Eliza? Can she go home?" It felt strange and sweet somehow to speak about Eliza, for it seemed most surely after all that had passed that night, and as we rode now through the snowy skies, that I had left her long ago. Perhaps some of my tender feeling had wormed its way into Captain Jane too, for her tone changed when she spoke.

"Not without your help, my love. That is the sad and sorry truth of it."

"But can't you help her? It seems like there is nothing you and your cloak and your boat cannot do. Won't Red Boy let you help her? You are so strong. You can do what you want. You struck Granny Someone from her chair. You took her place and worked that clever mercy. You are the strongest of all!"

"I have grown strong, it's true."

"You could knock Red Boy from his chair as you knocked Granny Someone and the singer from theirs!"

"Silence now, little love. You don't know what you speak of. Red Boy can't be knocked from any chair. It's Red Boy does the knocking. Red Boy already knows my wishes; he knew them long ago. There are rules to follow. Rules that govern all."

"I thought witches didn't follow rules."

"And I told you that I don't know what witches are."

"But you are a witch. You howl and kill and fly through the night."

"And so I should perhaps strip off my clothes and tear at my breast and mutter curses and take up a cat for my friend and go slinking about in the dark?"

"You do know what witches are."

"I know those stories, yes, for I haven't always belonged to the woods and I begin now to go abroad again. But they are poor little stories. Chanted in secret in the vain hope of knocking the hats off men. It's children shake their limbs in tantrum and smear themselves with mud and wander without reason and boil up potions and gibber at the moon and think it answers their call. We in the woods have our Red Boy, and the games we play are grand."

She said this and then down we plunged like a blunt-nosed shark through the banks of cloud and I saw that we had left the sea far behind and that now we skimmed treetops, then fields, then the stream that ran its quiet way beside my house. Captain Jane brought the boat to settle near our barn. She did it neatly. She asked me had I liked my boat ride and our play together at the house of the handsome singer and our run through the trees and my dive down the well, which was but a taste of what the woods had to offer. I said I had, for it was true, all of it was what I had ever desired. So deeply desired as I walked quickly through the dark with my father, both of us carrying our bundles, both of us spilling color. "It's a great world lies before us, daughter," my father said as we went tripping and stumbling and laughing. "It's deep and dark and grand and we'll ride the high mast and stitch our names into its sails." Down the dark road we ran, shouting our names and even screaming them, and it was nothing but fair salt wind to be felt and smelled and tasted until, when the bustle of the harbor could be heard and the ship he had arranged our passage on was in sight, my father stumbled in the swamp of his weakness and began to speak of the liniment my mother would rub into his shoulders when he was weary and the sweets she would sometimes slip into his mouth when it was just the two of them after her visits to town. I yanked up his sleeve and showed him the marks from the switch he still bore from her punishment by the water but he said she always spread ointment upon them afterward, that they always healed quickly and well. We must return to our home, to our great love, he said. We shouldn't have taken her treasure, which was all she had left from that earlier leaving. We must quickly gather it all back up. I begged him to keep walking. He said we would try our journey another night. Angel, angel, angel. Devil, devil, devil. Captain Jane slid open the boat's door. Snow lay deep across our yard.

"Who is Red Boy?" I asked.

"Ah, you're a one for questions, aren't you?" Captain Jane said. "You must have driven your parents mad." She gave me a little shove, like the one she had given me in the town and that first night in the forest, only this time it almost pitched me forward out of the boat and into the snow. But the hand that had shoved was quick enough to catch too and it pulled me back toward her.

"'Who is Red Boy?' she asks. Do you want to know who Red Boy is, my dear?"

"Yes," I said.

"Are you sure?"

"Yes."

She threw her arms wide and her head went back to laugh and, on a fancy, I took that moment to lean in close and put my ear against her chest.

"What are you doing? Have you gone soft? Do you wish now to cuddle with Captain Jane? I would advise against that!"

"I am listening to your heart," I said.

"Ah, I see, another kind of question. And what do you hear?"

It took me a moment to be able to say, for I had heard such a thing, but only long ago, when we lived by the water and a hurricane roared in to ruin buildings and sink ships.

"The center of a storm," I said.

"Of a great storm, yes. That's just right. The kind of silence that will crack your legs and shatter your ears."

Her arms snapped shut around me and I stood completely covered by her cloak.

"This is yours, love," she said and pressed something smooth and rough with a hole in its center into my hand.

"It's the bark! But I thought it was lost by Eliza's swamp."

"Eliza's lake, you mean, for that's what she calls it and so that is what it is. I told you I have been watching. Captain Jane finds things. Think of all that's come to you. A dead man's tear, fresh berries, and now this bit of black bark to help you see clear or crooked as you like. You've had a rich harvest with Captain Jane this night!"

I slipped the bark into my pocket, let it lie there with the berries. I touched at my fingertip with my thumb and could feel the tear.

"A rich harvest," Captain Jane said again. She blew on my cheek like she had blown on the face of the handsome singer. My skin burned hot where her breath had touched me. She blew on my other cheek and it burned too.

"If I blew harder, love, your skin would bubble and melt and fall in pieces onto the floor of this boat."

I tried to pull away from her but she held me tight.

"Now look this way," she said. We both looked toward my house. She blew in its direction and the air before us fizzed and steamed. She blew again, harder this time, and melted a deep trough in the snow straight up to my door.

"Blow with me," she whispered. I said I wouldn't and she said, "But I thought you liked to listen to hearts and play at games? I thought you wanted to know who Red Boy was . . . blow with me!"

"I won't," I said again, but I did. We blew in the direction of my house and more snow melted and seemed even to stop falling from the sky. The front door of my house began to glow and when we blew again, the roof burst into flame. *I must fetch my boy and warn my man,* I thought, but I didn't move; I blew. The air itself began to burn then, and soon the house entire and the barn beside it was a ruin of roaring, jagged red.

"Blow now like you mean it, my love," Captain Jane said and I blew, harder and harder, and the ground itself lit and the trees beyond and the air of the night and the night itself, it seemed, and I knew that Captain Jane had stopped blowing, that it was just me, that I was at the ending of my own great tale, that I had lit the world with its telling and that we would soon burn along with it and make of ourselves a burning, blazing suffix to the sun.

Captain Jane had turned back to face me. I looked and could see the roar of the world's great fire in her eyes.

"We'll burn it all, by the end. You'll see. Whether in a hundred years or three."

"I want to burn it now."

"I know you do."

"I am no goodwife."

"And never were."

The air was aflame. The clouds above us had been scorched away; the very blackness that blanketed the stars was roaring.

"That's a game, is it not?" Captain Jane said.

"Is it a game?" I asked.

"And part of the answer to your question."

As soon as she had said this, the glow in Captain Jane's eyes and the glow all around us was gone. The snow fell through the dark air and lay heavily on the ground. My little house sat waiting.

"And now," she whispered, "if you want to learn more about who Red Boy is, go back to beautiful Eliza, deary. Go back to the woods. But if not, run along and leave us who dwell among the trees to the shackles of our rules. Warm yourself at your own small fire and find your man and your son and eat your berries together and say your prayers and live your life and let it be easy and long."

"And what will happen to Eliza if I don't go back?" I whispered in return.

"Oh, you'll go back."

She pushed me hard away into the snow then. She clapped her hands and the boat leaped into the dark.

CHAPTER 23

I PICKED myself up from the snow and watched until Captain Jane and her boat of bones were gone then turned and, though my house no longer burned and was black but for a faint flickering through the parchment-covered windows, it warmed me to see it. I have twice in my life taken hard spirits and each time they spread heat from the tips of my fingers to the calluses on my feet and for all my house looked small and cold, I felt the same effect as I gazed at it, as if at least at its edges it really had begun to burn. I started forward only to stop a moment later when I caught a glimpse of the rabbit skull still hanging from its thread before the barn door. Seeing it, I felt an urge to visit our milking cow, whose warm cream I would serve with the berries I had brought, and also our sheep and our goat, to stop a moment and stroke their flanks and pat their bumpy heads and talk to them in the quiet of the barn. I stepped under the skull, pushed open the door, and started in. The cow heard me straightaway, as she always did, and started to call. This woke the sheep and soon the goat was bleating too. The noise seemed such a happy one to me that I all but ran to it and didn't see what was hanging from a rope in the clear space at the center of the barn. I didn't see it until I had made my way through the noisy gloom to the milking cow and had begun stroking her shoulder and flank.

My man had tied the rope under the dead owl's wings and stretched them wide and held them apart with a stick. As I stroked the cow's flank and pulled over a milking pail and began to tease and tug, the owl spun slowly around and I thought of my man's cleverness. A rabbit skull was nice if it worked some good charm, I thought as I pulled gentle-hard and my frozen fingers began to warm and hot milk to steam and squirt in the pail, but no pigeon or wood bird would roost in a barn with a great owl hanging from its center beam. The owl might rot to its bones, but even those bones would keep the smaller birds away.

"Just a few drops, girl," I told the cow and gave one last quick tug and squeeze with each of my hands. I had ever been good at milking and was loved by cow and goat both. My man said I had a softer touch than anyone he had ever known. He liked to watch me milk. Sometimes both man and boy would sit and watch. My husband's hands were far too large and hard for such work. I wondered how they had managed while I was away, for the cow was not in pain. Perhaps my man had found a way to teach our small boy. Perhaps they had prayed together about it. I had tried to teach him but our boy had run off quickly each time. I wondered at the shot my man had used to bring down the owl. How far away he had stood. Half a league away, it might have been. He was as good at shooting as he was at thinking.

With my man's cleverness in mind, I licked my lips and brought one of the handsome man's berries up and into my mouth, then I hefted up the pail and left the milking cow and her fellows with a good pat each and made my way by the horse shed to the house. I passed my early garden as I went, sure that most of the sprouts were still safe in their earth, then I passed the shed and I passed the woodpile. At last, I tried our door but it was latched tight. Thinking I might slip in one of the windows and save waking my man and my son so that when their eyes came open they might beam and leap about in happy surprise, I stepped over and peered in through a crack in the thin parchment and saw my man at the table by one of our lanterns.

He was asleep with his head on his arm so his face was turned toward me. His beard had grown wild in my absence and his mouth hung open and in the shadows of the lantern, it looked as though there were a hole punched deep into the floor of his face. Even with the window shut tight I could hear him snoring. When he had smoked and drunk he could snore loudly enough to break down a door. He did not look, as he lay there, like a man who knew the ways of mosses or like the man who had killed the owl then stretched and trussed it up so neatly. Nor did he look anything like the handsome singer either before or after he had made his acquaintance with Captain Jane's knife. I tried the window but it too was latched tight. I went around to the back of the house and found the windows closed there also.

There was one window left, on the far side of the house, and this one came open with a push. I put the steaming pail through the opening and climbed in, careful of the bark and berries. I brushed the snow off my dress and tiptoed into the front room. My man lay still and there was a stink in the house, which meant buckets needed dumping and rinsing at the stream. I went to the sundries room, where my man had spread a pallet of straw for me. The rope he used to tie my wrists hung limply over it from the wall post. I crept into our sleeping nook and found our boy buried under the blankets. He had always slept on his own pallet and, apart from the bitterest nights, had never been allowed in our bed before I left. I couldn't decide if I should thump my husband on the shoulder and ask him what this meant or thump my son. Perhaps I should thump them both. The ropes above the straw pallet in the sundries room had been rigged because lately I wandered in the night. The ropes were there because lately in my sleep I said and did things that my man couldn't understand. He had found me, for example, up to my ankles in the stream scraping with a stick on its murky floor. When he had asked me what I was doing there in the cold dark I had looked at him without seeing and said I was writing the Lord's good prayer. Another time he had woken to find

me painting my arms and legs with what I told him were letters, using mud and a brush I had made of hair I had cut from
his horse's tail. Often he woke to find me staring down at him
and more than once he had found me sitting by our son with my
mouth close to his ear.

My man had carved *Lie still or He shall smite thee!* into the
wood above the ropes and, when I wouldn't obey, had taken our
boy and ridden two long days to fetch the holy scarecrow who
had married us. My man had paid for the scarecrow's services
with as much cider as he could drink and the promise of a tenth
share of our next crop. The scarecrow had slept the nights he
spent with us on the floor beside me in the sundries room. I
had not slept during his visit for I knew this scarecrow and his
wandering hands too well, had known him my whole life. Each
time he woke in the night and saw me watching him carefully
he had said a prayer of his own making in which God was a
shield and Jesus a hammer and the Holy Ghost a heavy, cleans-
ing rain. When after the third night I had still shown no signs of
being, in his way of saying it, a horse in the night for the Devil
to ride, the scarecrow had bowed and smiled. He had offered
up a great, long prayer of parting, then lashed a jug of my man's
cider to his saddle.

My man believed I was cured then, and so the fourth night
too I went to bed, though still in the sundries room, untied. This
was after my boy had danced with his new shoes in the mud.
Into the dark of the house I rose. As asleep or not asleep as I

had been in the deep hours at Eliza's house. I took what was left in my mother's old chest and dumped it out onto our dusty floor. "Devil, devil, devil," I made the scraps of cloth say. "Devil, devil, devil!" I yelled at my son and at my man and, after they had woken, at the whole world. I went on yelling long after my husband had thrown as many of the scraps of cloth as he could into the fire then turned me out of the house. He said I could sleep that night beneath the rafters of the barn like the beast I had clearly become. I slept instead beneath the stars by the stream. It was there I remembered it was the time for spring berries and that I might find some to bring home with me if I looked carefully in the woods.

I've kept my promise, I thought. My son's little hand peeked out from the blanket and I saw there were light scrapes on it, as if he had been in the brambles. He had a thumb's smudge of dirt on his temple. His hair was wild and his scalp looked raw. I leaned over close and kissed him on his hand, then on his dirty temple. I caressed his cheek and sought the words to sing the song I had made up for him by the stream. I pinched him tenderly so that his eyes came open, and I pulled the little bit of berry-damp bark from my pocket.

"Here's a present for you, my darling," I said. "It came from a pretty little girl I met while I was away. I do not need it, for my own eyes are keen, and soon or someday I will learn to see in other ways. When you want to see a thing as it is or it isn't, you can look out through its hole."

My son took it from me and held it but not to his eye as I told him he should and instead went to licking stupidly at his lips, and straightaway I thought of how slow he had ever been with any new thing and clicked my tongue and wondered if he had even understood me.

"I just burned you and the whole wide world to a pile of cinders in a game!" I said. "I've played so many games since I left!" I pinched him again, not so tenderly this time, but then I thought of my song with its pretty words and phrases and calmed myself and took in my breath to sing it to him. Before I could make the first few sounds, though, he had sat up and bit my hand, then, still clutching the piece of black bark, he ran out past me to the other room. When I got up to follow him I saw that he had drawn blood.

"I will tan you for that, little devil!" I said. "I'll tan you then send you to live at the bottom of a staircase I know!" All in a fury I flew across the room toward him but stopped short when I saw he had crawled up into his sleeping father's lap. He had crawled up and, after smiling sweetly at me and tucking the bark into his shirt, he closed his eyes and fell back asleep. Or pretended to. They looked like peas in a pod then, did my son and my man, except that one was smaller and had a bulge of black bark in his shirt and the other was snoring and had a great filthy beard. I watched, with our house ticking in the cold, as my man leaned back a little in his chair, wrapped one of his arms around my son, and pulled him snug.

It was when my man shifted that I saw the grease-smeared knife on the table next to my two sleepers. Now this was a knife to be reckoned with. Much larger and longer than Captain Jane's. I had often stared at it so wherever it lay. It seemed to travel around the house, to turn up under pillows, upon the lintel, sunk up to its handle in the garden's dark earth.

The light of the guttering lantern played along its greasy length and I thought of sending my burning breath through the air with Captain Jane and how a fire was a kind of knife and could take so many shapes and forms. I found now that it was before me again that I had missed this knife of mine and longed to use it, as I had longed to in the dark beneath the stars before I had taken up my berry basket and left on my walk. I had swum down a well and flown through the air and set the world to roasting, but a sharp blade is its own sweet journey. There is nothing like your own knife, nothing in this world, and as I stood there, I even squeezed at the air as if I were grabbing it. I reached out again, felt the cold air touch the wound on my hand, noticed the slick blood on my thumb and fingers. *Stay where you stand, deary,* I thought, but I crept right to the edge of the table, leaned over, and peered closely at the knife.

Peering at it, I thought to take it up and plunge it quickly into my two sleepers as I had plunged it into my mother again and again for having danced on my father's grave and later laughed about it. Danced, then laughed after she had all but put him in his hole for suffering too loudly from a cough. She had not used her switch on that occasion; she had used the broken leg of the chair she had years before used me to break. My father had always promised to fix it and never had. She had made him stand though he was sick, and she had made him run though he could not, and then she had caught him with a laugh and beaten him and left him lying on the cold ground. She had done this and I had done nothing even though by then I was grown enough to have tried at least to stop her. I had sat fixed as the frost on our windows as she chased him from the house. She had called him back in afterward and told him not to whimper so and finish with his coughing and made me tend to him. This was not long after our return from his plan for us to climb aboard a ship and sail away to the place where kings still lived. She had sniffed it out, I thought. Or he had told her. Probably he had told her. "See what you have wrought for us, dear Father," I whispered to him.

Near the end he called me close. He said he wished to speak about my mother, our great love. I expected strong words at last, some curse. Instead, through the porridge in his chest, he croaked, "You must be the kind one now, as I have always tried to be."

He wept. I have never since known a man or a woman so weak, unless it were myself, and later wondered, as I plunged the knife into my mother, who it was I truly wished to stab. I had not stopped plunging the knife, which I had taken from my mother's own kitchen as she sat herself coughing next to

174

the fire, for some good while. She had stood the moment before to show my small son the dance she had made on my father's grave. "Don't show him that!" I had said. She had shown him then the bits and shreds of cloth she had taken with her to the churchyard to taunt him, who could no longer hear, and me, who stood by weeping, for our foolishness in imagining we might run off. "Don't show him those!" I had said. Then she had made my son smile by flinging them, as she had on that day at the cemetery too, over and over, into the air. "Goody!" she said to me, though she knew I hated to be called it. "Goody, see how he smiles! See how he likes my treasure." I watched as she caught up pieces of the cloth and made a trail of bits and shreds on the floor. "He's like you, Goody, and your poor fool father!" she said. "See how he follows the path I have made; see how he comes to me! See how he knows his place! See how he belongs first to me and then to heaven. Just like you!" With these words, her cough caught her and brought her down again into her chair and she began straightaway praying and I thought, *This is one prayer too many.* I had been preparing spring berries to eat with milk from my mother's cow. I fed my mother a berry. She spat it out, said it needed sugar. I told her I would fetch her some. When my man came home, we buried her in the barley field. I kept her old treasure and other things I thought she should have long since given to me. I told my man it was all mine now. He said after prayer that night that the dark one must have come to call. He held me with one hand and cuffed me with the other until I could barely stand and then said they'd have us both for the murder and that we must go far away. The next day we packed and left. We came here.

Where I stood, staring at the greasy knife. I didn't touch it. Instead, I set the pail of milk on the table, returned to the words carved by my husband above my pallet, and, using the blood on my hand for ink, made my fingertip into a quill and made it mean what now seemed true. Then I returned to the table and emptied the contents of my pocket into the pail.

"There's breakfast, boys," I whispered. "I'm sorry it took me so long. I thought of you often when I was away. I thought of you when I was in the water. I thought of you when I was in the sky. I thought of you when I sat in a cellar. I thought of you when I did not die." I spoke to them both but leaned ever closer to my little boy as I whispered these things. His breathing was soft but clear. "Don't be weak, my boy," I whispered. I know he heard me. It was something I had told him many times. But what did I mean? For I did not want him to be strong either. Not like his father, who could fling his cousin through the air. Not like my mother, who could chase the husband, who so loved her, with a switch. I meant some other thing. Something like Captain Jane in her wolf cloak. Something like Eliza when the metal was in her voice and she had set her jaw.

"Don't be weak," I said again and kissed my son on his soft cheek. When I did I saw my man's eye twitch, just a touch, so I knew he was awake too. I did not touch the knife. I breathed in deeply. I had smelled fear on my man before—of course I had—when I had walked our house in the dark, but rarely like this. I looked at the side of his great, filthy head.

"Ask me to stay," I told him. His eye twitched again. I brought my face very close to his. "Ask me nicely to stay and see how I answer." I waited. I told him I had held a quill and used it to write. I told him I had fed my name to a pig. I told him that if I stayed, he would have to dig me a deep cellar to do my scribbling in. That he would have to give me baths and scrub my nails because, devil's blood or not, from now on they would always be black with ink. My man said nothing but his great arm on the table began to tremble and his giant's hand to jump. "Is that your answer, husband?" I said. I thought I heard them both sigh when I went over to the wall and took down my coat. It was only unlined cow skin but sturdy enough, now that my dress was near dry, to see me through the cold.

CHAPTER 24

IT WAS a long walk through the deep snow and then the dark of the woods where the snow did not fall. My hand hurt and my legs were weary but soon the sun rose and shone weakly through the trees. Many times I wished that Captain Jane would come and whisk me up and away but then night fell and I still had not come to Eliza's house. Once I thought I glimpsed Granny Someone's cottage and began to breathe quickly but I calmed myself by remembering how deeply Granny Someone now slept.

Near dawn I saw a lonely glow a way off through the trees and before long the little girl in her yellow dress slid out from behind a stand of mulberry. Her eyes shone brightly in the light of the candle she was holding and she laughed prettily at my expression of surprise. She came over to me, gave a curtsy nice as you like, planted the candle she was holding in the ground beside us, and untied the laces of my shoes. She helped me slip them off, then picked her candle back up, stood, and offered me her hand.

"What is *your* name, child?" I asked her. "Do you have a strange name like the others who live in this woods?"

She would not answer. So we left my shoes behind and as we walked along holding hands I told her that I had a boy much her age and that I had given him the black bark. This made her nod exactly as if I had told her something that surprised her not one bit.

"Did you already know that I gave that piece of lovely, tricky bark to my son?" I asked, tugging playfully at her hand. "He'll stare through it until it gobbles up his eye, he will. Who knows what it will teach him."

She said nothing to this either, though now and again she smiled at me and her smile there in the woodland moonlight was a bright and beautiful thing.

"Are you a witch, like Captain Jane? Like Granny Someone? Do you belong to Red Boy?" As I asked this I saw Eliza's stone house, beaming brightly through the trees.

"I am Hope and belong only to myself," she said, looking sweetly up at me.

I laughed then and tousled her hair for it seemed most marvelous that there should be this little bit of hope here at the end of my long journey. I told her this and she smiled and said that it was just so, that even in a wood as dark as this one, there was always hope. She said that once I was settled in my new home she would come to see me. If ever I grew lonely I could call to her from my window or from the edge of my clearing into the trees. If I could not call I could bang on my window frame with a cup. I said that it wouldn't be *my* window or *my* clearing or *my* cup and that I could never be lonely with Eliza there, but I would call to her for it would please me always to see her and to think of her, like Eliza, as my friend. I also said, for it came quick upon me, that I wished my boy would speak, and speak when he did as nicely as she did, instead of scratching and biting when I only wished to hold him or help. I might never have left my house, I said, if it were her I'd have had to leave behind!

"I am not always sweet," she said. "Sometimes I sting."

"Hope's sweet sting. There's a song could be found in that. Perhaps I'll make you a song. Would you like that?"

She nodded. I felt when she did that she was starting to lag and saw now that there was a glaze over her eyes such as children who have stayed up too long are burdened with.

"Your feathery feet have turned to lead!"

"I have run too much of late."

"And now you're tired."

"Yes."

"And wish to sleep."

"I do."

"And what will you dream of when you've shut your eyes at last, dear Hope?"

"Of you."

I liked this answer and apologized for having gone on and on and told her I could carry her if she liked, that I would bear her carefully in my arms and help her in any way I could and try to be a good friend to her, but she just smiled wanly and looked back into the woods. When I saw that she would come no farther, I bent and kissed her soft forehead, just as I had kissed my son's. As I took my lips away and leaned back, she held her candle out to me.

"I can't take your candle, my darling."

"I brought it for you, Goody. To light the last of your way."

"But you'll need it, won't you?"

"I see well in the dark. I see perfectly."

"Stay with me and I'll make a song for you."

She shook her head.

I found a little tune and tried to make the song, but after "Of Hope's sweet sting / In dark night sing," nothing came, and she told me I could sing her the rest of my song another time.

"Good-bye, then," I said.

"Good-bye, Goody."

"I'm not Goody. Not really."

"That's true," she said.

I watched her leave, then, holding my fingers cupped around the candle's fragile flame, I walked the last small distance to Eliza's to see what it was I would see and learn how it was I could help.

Eliza's house, lit as always to greet the coming sun, grew brighter as I approached. I felt my spirits, already buoyed by Hope's company, rise into my chest, into my throat. Higher.

Higher still. With Eliza's tidy home at last before me, I thought not of my man or my boy but of my terrible mother in a moment of kindness and calm. Returned home the evening I escaped the handsome man, my mother carried me about our house, insisted I sleep in her lap, said I must never leave her arms. In the morning, after our breakfast, she took me up again and carried me into our yard in time to see a troop of soldiers in their bright red coats come past.

"Do you see how they march in a procession?" she asked. "Do you see how they march all in a line? This is God's good work before us. For that is how you hold the shape of your soul in its parcel. That is how you keep the pendulum swinging straight as you wind your clock."

"But we have no clock, Mother," I said.

"I had a clock before I came to live with your father. I had so many things and they are all gone."

"Except your treasure."

"Except my treasure."

"Where is Father?"

"He is off weeping for his sins."

"Do I have a soul, Mother?"

"Yes, of course, but it's not yet wrapped neat like the soul of those fine red soldiers walking by. We'll see it wrapped soon."

"I would like to hear a musket, Mother."

"And so you shall, my darling."

"I would like to hear a cannon, Mother."

"And so you shall."

"What will it sound like?"

"Like God's mouth opening at the start of your greatest day."

And here is the day set to dawn at last, dear Mother, I thought. Thinking of her and of all the burden I had now left behind and the black that would soon be always under my fingernails, I did skip and I did dance. *I should cry out,* I thought, for Eliza loved it so, and if I cried she would know I had returned and come out to greet me with her arms held open and a warm kiss at the ready. *I will help her,* I thought. *And repay the fault I earned in running off.*

I cried out. The cry caught in my throat, so I cleared it and tried again. It was not much of a cry and I thought Eliza would not think it fine or even recognize who had made it, so I stopped and closed my eyes and clenched my fists and took in my breath and kept taking it in until my shoulders were like wings for my ears, and when I opened my mouth I heard my own cry and thought it was the sound of the night and of the woods, of moss groaning and feet bleeding and the air burning.

I opened my eyes. And now all that had been bright was dark, as if my cry had robbed the world of its light. Bats and night birds moved through the air around me. There was a smell of death and a large lump in Eliza's yard. When I stepped closer and held out to no purpose the extinguished stub of candle in my hand, I saw it was the gutted corpse of one of Eliza's pigs, the great brown sow that had stood and turned to dance with her fellow. I did not need the bark nor even little Hope's light to see things clearly. What was left of the pig's entrails lay strewn about like the veins of a monstrous leaf let to fall and then to rot. The ground was slippery and warm. I felt my bare feet grow sticky as I walked across it. To Eliza's door. I put my hand on the latch and—softer this time, more gently—made my cry once more.

When I had my answer, which was nothing more than a quiet "Come in, Goody," I pulled on the latch and pushed open the door. It was dark when I started to push and bright when I stopped; the house had lit itself again with its roaring fire, its merry lanterns, even the stub of Hope's candle. I saw Eliza first, sitting at her table, small and kind and all that I had hoped for—a friend for this earth, for these long days—then pushed open the door farther and saw that she was not alone. Sitting beside her was my friend the robin. My friend and Hope's. Only grown great and hulking with the arms of a human creature, arms as large as my man's, as my mother's. His beak was sharper and his feathers redder than they had been when he was small. Before him, dropped directly onto the table, was raw meat from the pig. He let his thick arms hang heavily at his naked sides as if he did not yet know how to use them. I gasped but did not otherwise flinch and my little friend grown great sent his head down hard at the table to peck at the meat, to lift and—gurgling, showing me his huge red throat—swallow down gobs of it.

"I am happy you came back, but you should run away, Goody, my love," said Eliza. She smiled at me. In all my days since, I have never seen a sweeter smile. Nor a sadder, except in those rare moments when I have been brave enough to look in the mirror and gaze upon my own face.

"But I have come to help you," I said.

"You would help me?" she said.

"I have left my home now of my own desire, for having kept my promise I quickly saw that home was not what I wanted and I feared what I would do if I stayed. Captain Jane has shown me the kinds of things you can learn if you live in the woods. I have walked through the night and the day to come back to you, Eliza."

I put my candle on the window ledge by the front door, where it winked happily away. Eliza smiled her smile again and gave a small sigh that ended in a shiver.

"You must run home, Goody," she said. "For this is not a game one joins in lightly."

"I will not go home. I will never go home again," I said.

"You say that now," she said.

"I will say it always." As I told her this, I saw my husband's hairy face. I remembered the stench of him after he had been at the cider and the stench of my former home. I did not think of my little boy with his sharp teeth and soft cheek, though, for I knew despite all, if I did I might weaken in my resolve.

"Still, I say that you must run, my love, for now that I see

185

you sitting here again at my table, as much as I have hoped for it and dreamed of it, I find I cannot, indeed must not, ask you to stay."

There was more hard pecking at the pile of bloody meat. The room shuddered when the huge beak came down.

"I met our pretty friend in the woods," I said. "She spoke to me and told me her name. It was she gave me that stub of candle to light my last steps to your door. I wonder what she would say if she saw her little friend and mine grown grand and cruel as this."

"Hope has many friends. You will learn that if you try to leave before it's time or if anyone who shouldn't tries to visit you."

"I will not run, Eliza. I will stay and I will help you."

"You will miss your son. You may even come to miss your man."

"My son, yes, perhaps. But he is safer without me. I will never miss my man!"

I said this more loudly, I think, than was needed. Then I went outside, leaned over the sow, which had been neatly killed with a blow to the head, ferried up more gore from the open midsection, went back and dropped the steaming mess onto the table, and took my place again. Eliza and I sat quietly across from each other with the huge bird beside us. We might have been portraits, each of the other, our hair long and pretty, our hands stained red, her nails black and mine soon again to be.

Seeing our red hands together on the table I thought of the teardrop.

"Hold out one of your fingers," I said.

She tilted her head and looked at me but did as I asked. I reached out my finger and touched its jelly tip to hers.

"What have you given me, Goody?" she said.

"A gift. The last that I have. In case you ever need it. Perhaps you can use it when we are down in the cellar. You said that there were none of these left in your head."

"I did say that."

The tear slid under her nail and hid there. If the great bird had marked what had passed between us, he gave no sign, only smashed his head down, down and up. We watched him for a time, then Eliza sucked in her breath and spoke.

"You have come to this table and will stay and receive Red Boy's punishments and rewards both? Stay here and play this game? This game great and grand? You will do this to help me?" she said at last, looking long and carefully at me.

"I will not run for I do not fear him or his games. I do not fear your Red Boy, who takes his different shapes and tries to scare us," I said.

"See then what *I* have for *you*," she said.

She reached into the pocket of her own dress and pulled out the very scream I had fetched from the well and had last seen on the floor beside the handsome singer. She set it on the bloody wood between us. It jiggled a moment and went still.

187

Eliza stood then. She came around the table and put her hand on my shoulder. I saw that she was clutching a thick rolled bundle of her creamy paper. She squeezed my shoulder hard, then whispered sharp into my ear: "This giant bird is your Red Boy, not mine, Eliza. And fear him you *will*."

"But I am not Eliza. You are Eliza!" I said.

She gave me no answer, only made fast for the door. When I pressed on the table to try to rise and follow, Red Boy's head came down and he put his beak through the back of my hand.

CHAPTER 25

SHE GAVE no wild and pretty cry then. Only screamed. Her scream louder and longer, it seemed to me, than the first one I had made when my own Red Boy appeared. Her scream carried me out the door and sent me flying past my poor dead pig, which was now hers—stopping only long enough to snap away a tender bit of bone from one of its ribs—and across the yard. When I got to the edge of the woods I slipped the bit of bone under the string I'd used to wrap my quill-scratched pages. I pushed the bundle into my pocket and began to breathe more deeply than I had in years.

The scream followed me through the trees. Even when Captain Jane came and kissed me and welcomed me to what she called my "hard-won freedom," I could hear her screaming. Though when I told Captain Jane this, she said she heard nothing, that our friend might well be screaming, but what I heard was only the memory of my own scream trapped like a wasp in my head.

"It won't leave you, deary, it will never leave. Which is lucky for us, as there is much you can do in this woods and beyond with the sting of a remembered scream."

"Was I as loud in my screaming as she was?"

"I couldn't say. Perhaps not. Each scream is as different as each Red Boy. Different and the same. After you agreed to stay in my place, and your Red Boy came globbing and dripping from the walls, I left too quickly to listen, even more quickly than you just did. But this was a fine ripe scream, to be sure. Did you see how big it was? How big and juicy? It's been used a little but just enough to warm it."

"All she wanted was a kiss. I could have stayed another moment."

"You had already kissed her."

"A kiss when you want it is better than anything."

"Well, she's there now and you're here, free. What is her Red Boy like?"

I shuddered. Captain Jane nodded. "Goody fetched her own scream?" I asked.

"She is no longer Goody. You know that."

"I did not like holding that scream of hers."

"I did not like to give it to you to hold. Her Red Boy should have fished for it. As yours and mine did. We could have all watched him and seen what he was like."

"I have never heard of such a thing. Diving to fetch your own scream."

"Nor had I. It took Granny Someone's cunning to have her do it but her own fool courage and strength at paddling to get it done. Perhaps we'll do it that way the next time."

"She did seem brave."

"We have each been brave."

"Thank you for helping me in this."

"Captain Jane always helps those who deserve it."

"Do I deserve it?"

"Of course you do."

"I did things worse than she has done."

"Who says what's worse? And how do you know all that she has done?"

"When you were Eliza, when it was me sitting where she is now, you tricked me to get me to stay."

"You were Eliza for many years but I was Eliza longer. My Red Boy was worn to an ember that lived beneath my eyelid. It never stopped burning. I'd have done anything to douse it. We're no different, you and I."

"I won't come back," I said.

"Of course not, deary."

"I won't. Not like you. Not like the others."

"Storm and still, knife and quill, we all say we won't and then we almost all of us sooner or later will." She said this with a laugh as if it were a small and light thing to say after all those screams—the new Eliza's, mine, hers, the others before—a trifle there in the morning sun.

We came to the well, where I untied the string and dropped first the bit of bone and then my bundle of pages. It struck me that the teardrop under my fingernail might as well be added to the brew, for I did not want or need it, but scrape and shake as I might, I could not make it leave.

"Take your nail in your teeth and bite hard. You'll be able to catch it with your tongue," said a hollow voice, and old Granny Someone herself came up beside me, put her own crooked finger on the mossy stone and peered over the edge, then up at me.

"Is it true she swam in these waters?" I asked.

"True as that tear that doesn't want to leave you, dear."

"You must have made her do it."

"I had no glamour left in me when she dove."

"None at all?"

"Only petals and leaves and a splash of my old song."

"Where has your glamour gone?"

"I've had it stolen."

"I'd never swim in these waters."

"Never is such a long time, Eliza."

"I'm not Eliza. Not any longer."

"I'll take that tear. You don't need it. It smells of death and should be mine, for it was me filled the foul pond from which it poured. Give it here."

"And yet now I think I'll keep it."

Granny Someone growled low and long at being refused,

but when, with Captain Jane's arm back around my shoulder, I turned from the well to leave, she came with us, muttering imprecations with every step. Captain Jane, she said, had stolen her things and now had even stolen the secret snacks and suppers that would have built her strength back. There was nothing like an almost-Eliza ripe with worry and fury to top up your strength. This had been a fine one! One little push and she had swum to the bottom of the well and not drowned and brought her own scream back up. Who had ever heard of such a thing?

"I almost had scream and supper both!"

"In the end you had neither. Now be still, sad creature," Captain Jane said, but the old thing just smacked her lips and on and on she muttered. This must have bothered Captain Jane for every now and again she would let go of my shoulder and use her fist to deal Granny Someone a great blow.

"Does Hope not come to walk me from the wood?"

"She's resting now for her work with Eliza in the days to come. Without Hope it will be over before it fairly starts. Can you imagine your early hours and weeks as Eliza without Hope?"

"What work does she do with Eliza?" I said it bitterly, for though at the beginning of my time in the woods, Hope had come often enough to visit, she had long since stopped skipping to me when I called and had punished me when once I tried to seek her. Even when I had chanced so lately upon her and held out my arms and thought she had come to kiss me as I gazed upon the prospect of my departure, she had grinned and looked straight past me. "She made my time in the house longer," I said and spat. "Handing out her tricky gifts of sight. Eliza saw something that scared her when we were down by the water and ran away."

"Where did she run?" said Captain Jane.

"Home," I said.

"Not home."

"Then where?"

"To the woods. To the well. To that old creature. To *me*. She saw what she needed to see. She saw what she feared. And who do you think it was sent her buzzy, shiny friends to fill the air and chase that fool holding her berry basket away? I hadn't seen him. Granny Someone never sniffed him out."

"Still," I said.

"Still what?"

"Still, what would it have cost her to comfort me one last time?"

We walked and sometimes there came a howling through the trees so I knew that the wolves were near and no wonder with Captain Jane wearing Granny Someone's cloak made of the skin of their king. I had not walked abroad in the long years I had been in the woods, but I had thought so often of the route I would take when I had my freedom, if ever it came, that I did not need Captain Jane to guide me. I had on my old shoes, and they fit snug, and when we came to the edge of the trees and the start of the plains and hills I must cross to travel back to my home, I knew my time of trial was truly over and did not pause. Granny Someone came out of the woods and limped awhile alongside of me through the melting snow as if she meant to follow.

"She has something for you," called Captain Jane.

"No, I don't," she said. But after Captain Jane had sworn to come and skin her where she stood, she opened one of her crooked hands and I saw in it the piece of crimson string I must have left on the edge of the well.

"Take me with you," she whispered once I had it in my pocket. But Captain Jane called her sharp and she hobbled slowly back to the trees.

CHAPTER 26

IT TOOK nearly a week to make my walk home to our house in the mountains. My husband gasped and fell to his knees when he saw me. Two heavy, sullen girls—tiny things when I had left on the walk I had not returned from—stopped only a moment in their work and stared. My husband had found another woman to come and live in my house and sleep in my bed but I soon saw her off. Word spread of my return but none of our neighbors would set foot on our land or give me greeting when I walked abroad.

I let this trouble me not one bit. There were ways aplenty after all to repay their rudeness. I had learned many things beyond cries and screaming and writing stories during the years I had been gone. My daughters gleaned soon enough that they must come quickly when I called, and by and by they asked me, with a hungry gleam in their eyes, what it was I did with the herbs I gathered and the special soups I cooked. I taught them many a small trick, enough to please them and vex others, and often they would lie close and speak to me and to each other in the quiet way I had shown them, by rubbing their fingers lightly, lightly against their palms.

When my husband asked me, as he sometimes did, where I had been gone all that time, I told him I had been away wandering the world. The world, I told him, was a grand thing as long as you stepped straight and kept to your course. If you did not, the world would hurt you. Or it would make you hurt yourself. He said he knew that already. I told him he did not know it in the way that I did.

I grew quickly fatter and in the evenings, after his long day outdoors, my husband cooked our meals and did the cleaning while our girls rubbed my feet. They were miserable at letters, as I'd been before I left, though when I took up the paper and pack of quills I'd made their father fetch for me in town, they came and sat beside me and leaned in close.

"Words can make a circle," I told them. "Words in a circle can set a page afire."

"Show us," they cried.

"Bring me ink," I said.

They took up a cup, went outside, and tore the head off a chicken, which my husband scurried out after them to pluck. I dipped my quill when they were back and wrote, *Said the wolf to the lamb, "Do you know who I am?" Said the lamb to the wolf, said the wolf to the lamb* . . . Taking turnabout at each word, with much stumbling, they then read this aloud and, when finished, said it was nothing but a children's rhyme and tossed it aside. A moment later, though, they shrieked with fear when they saw that the floor where the page had fallen had started to smoke.

They had all sunk deep into the habit of churchgoing and church-thinking in my absence and had often, my husband told me, said a prayer for me. Now they wished, he said, to offer up their prayers at church in my company. I said I would not go to their church but did not forbid them from frequenting it once each week themselves. My husband took advantage of this arrangement, which gave us both freedom, to convince the great, fat parson attached to the valley church to come all the way up to our house on the mountain to bestow upon me his blessing. Still, when this fat personage had ridden to the gate at the edge of our yard and had seen me standing in the doorway of our house with a pipe in one hand and an ink-stained quill in the other, he would ride no farther and, despite my husband's cajoling, quickly went away.

I was not pleased by this visit and made my husband know it and to further instruct him took my daughters with me the next morning in our wagon. I had at first no destination in my mind, just the desire to roll far away for a moment from house and husband. Fast in this desire we rolled, fast and faster, until we were flying almost through the air instead of over the ruts of the foul little lanes that led down out of the mountains. My girls smiled at our speed, for their father, they told me, always drove slowly, so slowly that they thought they might turn to stone or salt and die of age before a journey's end. We crossed no one as we left the mountains though saw many at a distance who, as we flew down toward them, wisely turned their mousy tails and ran. Spying them as they fled from us made me laugh and so my daughters laughed too for they attended me in all ways now. We laughed with our throats but spoke to one another as we flew with fingertip and palm, and tongue and mouth top, and in other ways I had taught them.

Always they asked me about where I had been during the long years of my absence and who had kept me safe. I told them that no one had kept me safe, that I had not been safe, that there was nowhere on this world or off it where we could be safe, not even for a minute. I tried more than once as we rode and as they looked into my eyes to tell them where I had been and what had happened there while I was kept but found each time I did that I could say only very little. A mist had settled over the images that twisted before my eyes, turning them, even as I could not look away, from memories of me to quill-scratched stories of someone else. Stories of Eliza. Another Eliza. The other Eliza. Eliza who was no longer me. My name had been Faith before, so it was Faith again. She was Eliza. All of it was hers now.

It was with visions of the new Eliza and her life in the little stone house floating before me that I found we had flown far from the mountains to the very edges of the great dark wood. I would have pointed at it to show them, but my girls had fallen sloppily asleep and their soft heads lolled each in its own way against me. I slowed the team but still we stepped fast around the fringe of forest, around the blacks and browns of the tall trunks and swaying branches, past the heavier blacks of the shadows beyond. By and by we struck a stream that trickled past the trees, and the horses, slathered in sweat, followed it. We rode along the edges of the stream for a time then came to a farm. In front of the farm's house was a boy. He was playing in a puddle. Leaping into and out of it. Even as I left my girls sleeping in the wagon and climbed down and crossed the stream and walked to him, he kept leaping in and out of his puddle. When I was almost to him he stopped suddenly and turned.

"Good day, child," I said.

The boy did not speak. He held his hands at his sides and dripped down puddle water from his waist and arms.

"Is this your house, child?"

He did not speak. A man came and stood in the doorway of the house and looked out at the boy. The man had a great beard and a fearful smile and told the boy to come to him but the boy did not listen; he looked at me. As I watched, the boy lifted the piece of black bark I now saw was hanging from a rope of colored cloth around his neck and brought it to his eye.

"What is it?" said the man. "What is it you see now? More of your goblins and fairies of the wood?" The man spoke kindly but with more than a flicker of worry. I called out a greeting to him but he neither looked in my direction nor responded.

"I see Eliza of the woods," said the boy.

He was looking through his piece of bark toward me.

"I am not Eliza, child," I said. "I dropped my coin and story in the well and left."

"I see Eliza and she is all bloody," said the boy.

"I am not Eliza, not any longer. My daughters are with me; they are in the wagon, and you see only what you wish and want. That bark plays tricks!"

"I see Eliza and she is all dark and she is pointing to the stream where lie two slaughtered pigs," said the boy.

"Your mother is Eliza, not me, not anymore. It is her turn now to dance a long day with her Red Boy, not mine!"

"Come now," said the man, stepping full out of the house and looking carefully around him. "Speak if there is something that troubles you. I know you can do it."

"He *has* spoken, Goodman!" I said. "Did you not hear him? Can you not hear me?"

The boy slowly let the piece of bark fall away from his eye to hang once more from his neck, jumped again into his puddle, sent glittering drops flying through the air and almost to me, then ran to his father. He took his father's hand and they went into the house.

"I am not Eliza, you have not seen her this day," I shouted after them. But neither turned so after standing there awhile, I walked away. The horses had found their path with the wagon to the muddy banks and were drinking as deeply as if they meant to drain the stream. My daughters would not wake. They were not pigs. They were not slaughtered. They were just great, glum girls grown bored with the day. I must have had the winds of the spell that had brought us so quickly down from the mountains still wrapped around my shoulders for the father not to have seen me and for the boy to have mistaken me so.

"I am not Eliza," I told my sleeping girls, and I found as I did, perhaps because they were not looking at me, not listening, that though I could not quite have said aloud what had happened to me, I could remember the rules I had long lived under, remember and speak them both.

"Eliza lives in the house in the woods. Red Boy lives there with her. She has long grown the image of Red Boy in the bloody soil of her heart and now he is sitting next to her and now he is ready to play. How he loves to play! How Eliza screams! In the beginning, Hope pays her visits, but then those visits slow and soon she doesn't visit anymore. Eliza lives a long time with her Red Boy without Hope. Some days and nights cost less than others, but Red Boy, even as he slowly grows smaller and smaller, is there for every one.

"Then Goody comes to the woods. Goody is young. Goody is clever. Goody has been bad. Only if Goody agrees to stay in the stone house may Eliza leave the game. Not all Goodys stay. Some learn what lies in store for them and flee. Some leave and return, leave and return, then leave and don't come back. Some are gobbled up in the wood by Granny Someone.

"When Goody finally takes her place, Eliza drops the tale of her long days down the throat of the woods to feed another scream. She becomes Faith, or Charity, or Virtue, or Prudence again and leaves the woods. She hurries home. She does not want to go back to the trees. If she goes back, she becomes a spirit and belongs to the woods forever. A spirit may become Captain Jane and help. Captain Jane may, if she is fierce, become Granny Someone and hurt and help as she likes. Red Boy is always Red Boy. Hope is always Hope."

I shook my girls by their thick shoulders. They did not wake. "I will not go back," I said. I did not say this to my sleeping daughters. I said it to the dark trees in the distance. After the horses had slaked their thirst I got them moving again, but they would not roll near so fast on returning. Once we hit a bump and my daughters' eyes came open. "Where does her Red Boy go when Eliza leaves the woods?" one of them asked me. "He vanishes," I said. "Like Hope," said the other. "Not like Hope," I said. "He stays much longer. It's only at the very end when Goody's Red Boy takes his place that Eliza realizes he's gone."

I looked up and off to the side as I spoke. I curled my lip. I squinted my eyes. I told them to lean close and have a listen. To see if they could hear him, to tell me if they could, that the heart he had sprung from had ever been his favorite place to rest and hide. When my daughters made no answer I looked down at them and saw that their own eyes had closed again and so deeply were they breathing I wondered if they had ever truly woken. The horses clopped on. Once upon a time there was and there wasn't a woman who came home from the woods. It was a long and wearying ride indeed before we saw our mountains again.

CHAPTER 27

WHEN WE were home at last and had put the horses to stable and splashed away the dirt of our journey and had eaten well of good cheese and meat, I sent my daughters away and went into the house and called my husband and bade him lie down upon our bed. I found my quill and tickled his cheek a little with it when I told him that if he obeyed me from now on all would be sweet between us. I tickled his chest too. I tickled his temple and left only, in each of these places, a very little bit of blood. I told him that if I had been strong before I left, I was stronger still now that I had returned.

I tapped my chest with the quill, then tapped his. I laughed when he winced, or tried to wince, and told him I had long since paid for what I had done to my sister, Glory, after he and I were first married, and she had come to visit us with her bastard child and to wink at my husband and laugh each moment out of jealousy and spite at my clothing, and at my cooking, and at my cleaning, to laugh at me who was well and married while she was discarded and disgraced. They had not departed for their home in the wee hours, as I had told him. They had never departed our land and I had paid for it each day for years in the dark of the woods.

"You will call me Eliza, not Faith, now, and never Goody, as you know," I told my husband. "For I was never your goodwife and was only ever Goody to the woods and to my rage.

"Call me Eliza now," I said and tapped his jaw with the quill.

"Eliza," he croaked.

I bade him sit up and press his ear against my chest and tell me what he heard.

"Nothing," he said.

I pushed him back down and tapped at his temple and saw as I did so that the teardrop that had been hiding so long under my nail had come loose and slid down the length of the quill to hang dripping from the tip.

"Say my name," I said as I tapped the tip of the quill, and the tear slid down his cheek then stopped in its falling and climbed back up and then fell again.

"Eliza," he croaked more loudly.

"And what did you say you heard of my heart?"

"Nothing."

"That's right."

I tickled him with the quill and kissed him long. When he started to groan I tapped his jaw and struck him silent again.

CHAPTER 28

CAPTAIN JANE came to see me in her boat the very next day. She seemed grown larger and grander by great measure and did not straightaway smile at me as she always had before. She told me almost with her first breath that it was not just a new Eliza and her Red Boy in the woods, that she was Granny Someone now. She wore her wolf cloak and floated just above me in her boat as she recounted how she had disposed of her predecessor just after I had earned my freedom. As soon as the old Granny Someone had stepped back into the woods, Captain Jane had stripped her of her last spells and few remaining spirits and set her to run.

Aged as she was, old Granny Someone led her on a merry chase that kept her busy the day long. Even without tricks and glamour, she knew the woods and its secrets better than any and it was only when Captain Jane pulled her cloak tight and felt her teeth turn into fangs and her arms and legs into engines for endless hunting and all the wolves of the woods press close that she ran her to ground. Indeed, they had cornered the old Granny Someone in the very caves below the earth she had been held in, when she was still called Goody, and had just slowly poisoned her overpreening younger brother to death with herbs and roots after he had inherited the house they had both grown up in and turned her out. Captain Jane had been for finishing her there in the cave, slowly, with great care, but the old Granny Someone had been wily and in the midst of all the barking and howling and whining and biting she had slipped free to reach the surface and run a little more.

Finally, she had sought refuge at Eliza's and that had put an end to their part of it. For of course they could not set foot on Eliza's grounds. Red Boy had emerged after a short while holding some of the new Eliza's bloody hair. All of them then had stood at the edge of the woods and looked into Eliza's yard and attended the demise of the old Granny Someone, who had clearly held on to her position for too long.

The new Granny Someone paused in her tale, as we both, I suppose, thought of our earliest minutes as Eliza and tried to remember how they had been. Indeed, she told me, she had stood with her wolf cloak loosened again and looked a good long while at the yard and at the house in which she and I and so many Elizas, including the one that lay in her final ruin before them, had lived. Then they had left that place behind and had all gone to dance and sport in the trees around the well.

The new Granny Someone asked me, when she had finished

telling me this, if I was ready yet to leave my dull family and mountain behind me forever, to put down my pipe and petty tricks and join them at their sport and play along the paths and in the glades. She could see the ink stains on my fingers and knew I was still scribbling out of old habit and wouldn't it be more fun to set aside my quill and go howling and galloping through the trees? The stains would stay, for dark stories lingered. I would soon weary of the few small conjuring tricks I had learned and wouldn't it be nice to learn more? *Much* more? Everything I had learned as I looked so long into the fiery eyes of my own fierce heart was just a start, a glittery shard. The scream had been a gift, Red Boy a glory, for where else in this world of towns and farms and crosses could great hearts roar? Even the smallest spirit who returned to Red Boy's woods could bunch her fists and bite. Once already I had made a trip in my wagon to look at the trees and pay visits to nearby houses and wouldn't I like to come back again and this time stay? A new Captain Jane was needed. Perhaps it could be me.

"You think you've lost all that lived in your chest," she said. "But come back to the woods and you will see. It'll bang so loudly, you'll beg me to cut off your ears."

She said this with a wink and a grin, and I thought of the boy in the puddle who had taken me for what I no longer was though perhaps still longed to be. I thought of my husband, whom I had not yet released from the bed, and of the tear rising and falling upon his face. I thought of my daughters and, poor conjuring tricks or no, of how much I had still to teach them. More than anything, though, I thought of Red Boy and of his play in the house with Eliza.

"You're wearing your red string," said Granny Someone. It was true. That morning I'd had my daughters tie it tight around my wrist.

EPILOGUE

WHEN THE snows were gone and the summer had come, a first-folk man brought us my mother's blue bonnet. When my father asked him where he had found it, he pointed over his shoulder past the stream to the woods. That night I rose from the bed, made sure my good mask of black bark hung safely from my neck, pulled my cloak down off its peg, and crept quietly past my father. Before I reached the front door I turned back, took the knife off the table where my father sat sleeping, and used it to cut free a piece of his beard. The knife was long and sharp and shone like the light of a star wrapped tight around a stick. I was not supposed to touch it. My father did not move when his beard was being cut. An empty jug of cider sat next to his arm. I put the knife back on the table and the piece of my father's deep brown beard in a pocket my mother had sewn onto the inside of my cloak.

I was halfway across the garden and out into the world when I turned around once more. I went to the table and took up the knife. I wrapped it in a piece of rag, then tied the rag with string, then kissed my father. The long hairs of his beard tickled my nose. My father did not move even when I kissed him again. There was another, larger pocket on the inside of my cloak. I put the wrapped knife into it and went to the place where my mother had slept her last nights in our house and ran my finger over the *s* she had added to the carving my father had made, then read it aloud: "'Lie still or sHe shall smite thee!'" The *s* was so faint now it was hard to see but I could see it. "Lie still, Papa," I whispered, then kissed him one last time, walked out the front door, and went across the garden to the barn.

The cow was in her stall and she lowed when I came in. I told the cow she should be sleeping and eating good grass in her dreams, then gave her a pat on her flank. The cow turned her head and looked at me with one of her great black eyes. The world was still very dark but I could see myself in the cow's eye. I had often played at pretending I lived in that eye. That I had a house there, and one in the nearby goat's green eye, and in the sheep's yellow one. I would move from house to house. No one could find me when I was in these houses. The house in the cow's eye was the biggest and safest. I did not need it now. "I have a knife and am going to find Mother in the woods and I will bring her home and I will not be weak," I said.

I stepped away from the stall and stood on the tips of my toes and took hold of the dead owl my father had hung from the barn rafters to chase away smaller birds. My father had found the owl dead in our field last spring and brought it into the barn. I had helped my father to stretch the dead bird's wings and strap them onto branches of wood to keep them open. Then I had helped to hang it. I stood tall and took hold and pulled off one of the owl's feathers. The owl did not smell fresh. When we had hung it, the owl had smelled like moss and softened tree stump and wet wool and the windy heart of the air. Now it smelled like the little animals that sometimes died beneath our house.

I said good-bye to the owl, then to the cow and to the goat and sheep, who were sleeping in their own stalls, then left the barn and left the yard and tucked the feather in my pocket and pulled my cloak tight and walked toward the stream. The stream was a sheet of stone in the moonless dark and I was afraid for a moment as I came to it that it might have died, that the creatures that lived where my mother had gone had found a way to kill it, as they sometimes came and killed me in my dreams.

But when I crouched beside the stream and tied my mask of bark tight across my face so that I could look through it with my best eye, I could see well and clear that it was still alive the way I wanted it to be. I touched at its waters with my fingers and felt its cold. Sometimes my father took me to the stream to splash but even then I was not allowed to cross to the farther bank. "I am not weak," I whispered. I stepped in. The cool, smooth stone of the water's surface softened and let me pass. Little fish woke but did not bite. My pants became heavy below the knees. The edges of my cloak dragged behind me. A frog sat on the far bank. I thought it might speak, tell me where I should go, point me straight to my mother, give me some good guidance, but it sat silent and closed its eyes, so I opened mine even wider. When day began to break, my way seemed clear. For as it rose, the good sun lit a line down the middle of the long field I found before me and seemed to set the air of the trees in the distance, and the whole wide world beyond them, to burn.

ACKNOWLEDGMENTS

This novel could not have been written without the sharp edits, sage advice, sustaining encouragement, inspiring conversation, cloth-rending performance, and/or timely reading and viewing recommendations of Eleni Sikelianos, Eva Sikelianos Hunt, Kathryn Hunt, Lorna Hunt, Stephen Hunt, Linda Wickens, Anne Waldman, Ed Bowes, Anna Stein, Josh Kendall, Nicky Guerreiro, Tracy Roe, Karen Landry, Clare Alexander, Lesley Thorne, Claire Nozières, Kate Bernheimer, Selah Saterstrom, Debra Magpie Earling, Susie Schlesinger, Ella Longpre, Nick Arvin, and Marion Laine. I thank you all.

The epigraph quote is from Edgar Allan Poe's "The Raven."

ABOUT THE AUTHOR

Laird Hunt is the author, most recently, of *The Evening Road*, which was a *Financial Times* of London best book of 2017. His previous novel, *Neverhome,* was a *New York Times Book Review* Editors' Choice selection, an Indie Next selection, winner of the Grand Prix de Littérature Américaine and the Bridge Book Award, and a finalist for the Prix Femina Étranger. He lives in Providence, Rhode Island, and teaches at Brown University.